W9-BMT-544

Like Water on Stone

DANA WALRATH

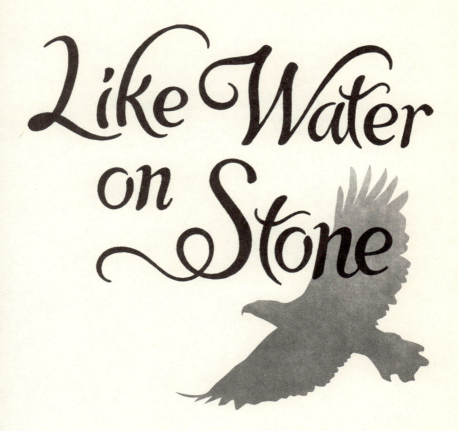

DELACORTE PRESS

Text copyright © 2014 by Dana Walrath
Jacket type copyright © 2014 by Sasha Prood
Jacket photograph © 2014 Shutterstock
Interior art © Shutterstock
Map illustration copyright © 2014 by Joe LeMonnier

Visit us on the Web! randomhouse.com/teens

Educators and librarians, for a variety of teaching tools,
visit us at RHTeachersLibrarians.com

Library of Congress Cataloging-in-Publication Data
Walrath, Dana.
Like water on stone / Dana Walrath. — First edition.
pages cm
Summary: Inspired by a true story, this relates the tale of
siblings Sosi, Shahen, and Mariam who survive the Armenian genocide
of 1915 by escaping from Turkey alone over the mountains.
ISBN 978-0-385-74397-6 (hc) — ISBN 978-0-385-37329-6 (ebook)
ISBN 978-0-375-99142-4 (glb)
1. Armenian massacres, 1915–1923—Juvenile fiction. [1. Novels in verse.
2. Armenian massacres, 1915–1923—Fiction. 3. Brothers and sisters—Fiction.
4. Genocide—Fiction. 5. Armenians—Turkey—Fiction.
6. Turkey—History—Ottoman Empire, 1288–1918—Fiction.] I. Title.
PZ7.5.W22Lik 2014
[Fic]—dc23
2013026323

The text of this book is set in 12-point Baskerville.
Book design by Heather Kelly

Printed in the United States of America
10 9 8 7 6 5 4 3 2 1
First Edition

To the survivors, to those who fell,
and to those who cross divides to prevent genocide

Where the needle passes, the thread passes also.
                                        —Armenian proverb

Cast of Characters

Ardziv (Ar-DZIV): An eagle

Donabedian (Doh-na-BED-ee-ahn) Family: Armenian family of millers in Palu, Western Armenia, 1914

Papa

Mama

Anahid (AH-nah-heed): daughter, age nineteen, married to Kaban's son, Asan

Misak (MEE-sock): son, age seventeen, works in the family mill with Papa

Kevorg (KEH-vorg): son, age fifteen, works in the family mill with Papa

Shahen (SHA-hen): son, age thirteen, twin to Sosi, studies with Father Manoog

Sosi (SOH-see): daughter, age thirteen, twin to Shahen

Mariam (MAH-ree-ahm): daughter, age five

Keri (KEH-ree): Mama's brother, lives in New York City

Their Community: Turks (Muslims), Kurds (Muslims), Armenians (Christians)

Bedros Arkalian (BED-ros ar-KAL-ee-on): clock maker, Armenian

Vahan (VA-han): Bedros's son, age sixteen; apprentice to his father

Father Manoog (MAH-noog): Armenian priest and teacher

Mustafa Bey Injeli (moo-STAH-fah bay IN-jel-ee): Papa's friend, a Turk

Fatima (FAH-ti-mah): Mustafa's wife

Kaban Ocalan (KA-bahn OH-jah-lan): Papa's friend, a Kurd; father-in-law to Anahid

Palewan (PAH-le-wahn): Kaban's wife

Asan (AH-sahn): son of Kaban and Palewan, age twenty-one; husband of Anahid

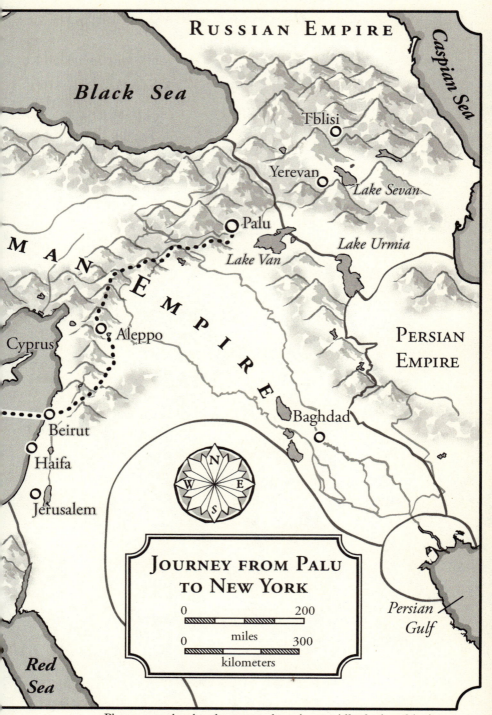

RUSSIAN EMPIRE

Black Sea

Caspian Sea

Tblisi

Yerevan

Lake Sevan

Palu

Lake Van

Lake Urmia

M A N   E M P I R E

Cyprus

Aleppo

PERSIAN EMPIRE

Beirut

Haifa

Baghdad

Jerusalem

N
W E
S

Red Sea

JOURNEY FROM PALU TO NEW YORK

0   200
miles
0   300
kilometers

Persian Gulf

Please note that borders were changing rapidly during this time.

I

PALU
1914

Ardziv

Three young ones,
one black pot,
a single quill,
and a tuft of red wool
are enough to start
a new life
in a new land.
I know this is true
because I saw it.

We track our quills
when they fall.
Always.
With eagle eyes
we can see
from the sky
who picks one up
from the ground,
or rescues it
from the crook
of a bent branch,
the quill's mottled color
blending in
with the peeling bark.

It was the girl
who picked up my quill.
She and her mother
worked side by side,
plucking frothy white
beetle bodies
from leaf and stalk.
They crushed them
between fingertips
and used this insect blood
to turn their carpet fibers
the richest red.
Clever.

When my feather dropped,
the girl, the older one, Sosi,
almost full grown,
her body budding,
stirred from her work.
The little one, Mariam,
napped on a carpet beside her.

Sosi, named for plane trees
that stand tall on this land.
Her short, quick inhale as she saw it
tugged the air around me.
She wiped her red-tipped fingers
on her apron before reaching up.
"Look, Mama, a new *mizrap* for Papa."

A nine-beat song
pulsed through my wings.
A musician?
What luck!

If my quill could pull laments
from the strings of an *oud,*
I thought, then
my heart might heal.
"That quill is for your brother,"
the mother said.
"It's time that Shahen
learned to play."
A young musician?
More luck.

Far beyond this beetled field,
where river cut through mountain,
a curly-headed, big-eyed boy
shivered when she spoke.
Shahen.
Sons hear as eagles see.

Fast green water flowed
along the distant bank.
An arc of giant stones
rose from the riverbed,
bending the current's
forward force.

Water seeped back
behind these stones,
forming a still pool
for Shahen,
his face reflected in the water,
so delicate,
like Sosi's.

His thumb and fingers
curled round
a flat, smooth stone.
He bent his hand
tight toward his arm.
One fierce flick of his wrist
sent the stone to water.
It skipped nine times
like the beat of a song.

Ripples spread
through the top of the pool,
then sank
into its surface.
Then, to no one,
to the air,
perhaps to me,
Shahen said,
"No one plays *oud* in America."
My musician, what luck!

Shahen

Come on, lucky stone.
Give me seven.
Not nine, not eight.
One for each of them,
none for me.

Papa,
Mama,
Kevorg,
Misak,
Anahid, Sosi, Mariam,

Me.

Eight? It can't be eight.
Not the eight arches
of the Palu bridge.
I can't be stuck here
with a fool for a father.
In a land ruled by Muslims,
priests just *baaaah* like sheep.
My fate isn't here, sitting in church,
learning of what was, not of what could be.
My fate isn't here, grinding wheat into flour.

That's enough for my brothers,
big dolts with no dreams.
Come on, stone. You're the lucky one.

Papa,
Mama,
Kevorg,
Misak,
Anahid, Sosi, Mariam,

Me.

Pah! Stupid eight.
Stupid, like Papa,
who keeps his head in song.
If he stopped playing the *oud*,
if he looked instead of listened,
if he stopped thinking we are all the same,
that Christians, like us, could ever be free
deep inside an empire
ruled by Muslim Ottoman Turks,
then he would know.
From the Balkans
to the Caucasus
and down both sides
of Arabia, they rule.
But other empires
close them in:

Austrian, Russian,
Persian, and British
meet them at each edge.

They have no place for us,
not in their hearts.
Papa should know this.
He was alive in 1895,
when Sultan Hamid
first gave the orders to kill us,
not me.
He knows we pay
double taxes
and cannot vote.

He knows Turks call us
gavour, infidel.
Now it will be even worse.
Armenian families will shun us
because Anahid's groom is a Kurd.
What sort of Armenian father
blesses a love match
with a Muslim
for his first-born girl?
So what if she didn't
have to convert?
It's Kurdish *beys*
who take the tithe.

If he opened his eyes,
if he stopped thinking
of the world as a song,
with disparate parts
always blending,
he would know
that my *keri*, my uncle, is right.
All the way
from New York,
Mama's brother
knows the truth.
We should marry
our own.

If I go to New York
to live with my *keri*,
my face will be bristled at last,
no longer the little one,
the little brother,
twin to a girl,
with a fool for a father.

There I'll grow tall.
The bristles will come.
I'll live in a tower
that touches the sky.

Come on, pink stone,
perfect, smooth, and flat.

Cut me out.
Make it seven.

Stone spins and cuts the surface.

Papa, big spray;
Mama, less;
Kevorg, closer;
Misak, smaller;
Anahid, Sosi, Mariam.

Stone sinks into water.

I will do it with care.
As the proverb says:
Measure seven times.
Cut once.
That's how I will do it.

I'm going to America.

Mariam

Feet up.
Feet down.
Heels hit house.
Feet up.
Feet down.
Shahen,
come home.

Time to play the bird game.
Time to play the bird game.

Feet up.
Feet down.
I sit.
I wait.
Feet up.
Feet down.
He's here!

Shahen's on the ground,
his arms spread wide.

"Time to play the bird game?"
"Yes," he tells me.
He always says yes.

My wings pull back.
Meg, yergoo, yerek,
one, two, three,
flap, flap, flap.
I fly.
My heart goes first,
down
down
down
from the roof
into Shahen's arms.
He catches me.
He holds me high.
He spins me
round and round
like the mill wheel.
I fly above.
I am his little dove.

Shahen

Fly, little bird.
Fly over hills.
Fly straight through the straits to the sea.

She giggles. We spin.
Her curls catch the wind.
My fingertips press to her ribs,
to help me remember her laugh
and the smell of the mint by the stream
and Sosi, on tiptoes,
stringing the loom with strong cotton cords,
tying tight knots at its base,
Mama rolling rice into grape leaves,
packing them snug
into the black pot to simmer,
my father and brothers dusted with flour,
their faces white like clowns
when the mill work is done.

From New York,
I will be able to see across oceans,
past pashas in Topkapi Palace
and drum-capped Ottoman soldiers,
their Muslim guns pointed toward our land,

through a maze of Turks and Kurds,
with Anahid among them,
to my family here in Palu.

I land Mariam
back on the roof's edge.
Her tiny feet kick.
She leans out again,
leading with her breastbone.

Meg, yergoo, yerek.

Ardziv

Built low to the ground,
this roof was safe,
even for those without wings.
The mill house roofs ran up the slope
like stepping-stones,
each roof set for its own tasks:
carpet making, laundry,
cooking, feasting, music.
Stone steps set tight
into outside walls
led up to all the rooftops.

That night, on the roof,
the father used my quill
to pull sweet sounds
from the strings of his *oud,*
its bulging belly nestled between his arms,
so like a young human mother
making room for a coming child.
Eggs in nests are far more simple.

His soaring sound pulled me from the sky,
like gravity must for those who can't fly.
I lighted on a branch near their roof.

The father stopped playing.
Beside him, Shahen lay on his back,
staring past me and the treetops.
The father reached down.
He touched Shahen's forehead
with my quill and said,
"This fine new *mizrap,* this gift from an eagle,
the noblest of birds, is a sign, Shahen.
It's time for me to teach you."
With the pluck of a young one aching to leave the nest
the imp rolled to his side and replied,
"No one plays *oud* in America, Papa."
"A good Armenian carries the music of home
close to his heart, wherever he is, son."
"You mean I'm going?"
I tipped my head under mantle of wing
lest they hear me whistle.

We eagles sing no soothing songs.
Our throats can only whistle.
Instead, we hunt them down,
take them from others.
I craved soothing song that summer.
I had lost my mate and hatchlings
and war was in the air.

Hate makes jagged spikes of light,
and blame can crack the sky.
As pierced with wounds

from sharp white teeth,
the Ottoman air had ruptured.
Massacres would come again
as the drum-capped rulers
spread their hate.

I confess. I had my own hate
for the drum caps that summer.
I kept it
like an egg in a nest,
warming it,
feeding it once it hatched,
so it grew ever stronger,
the drum caps' hate
like food for mine.

Before the time of humans,
we eagles had no need for hate.
We do not feign to own the land.
We keep it safe around our nests
from hawk and falcon
so that our young can fledge.
And to hunt is to fight,
is to kill, I know.
But its purpose is pure.
How else could we feed our young?

That long-gone night,
I stopped my distant flights

across this land of seas.
Instead, each day,
I flew over their mill,
built into a small stream
that fed the eastern branch
of the mighty Euphrates River,
hoping for snatches of music.

Sosi

Mama teaches me how
to bargain for fabrics.
First, fingertips feel
texture and weight,
face and voice silent.
Never take first price.
See what the Turks have to offer,
but buy Armenian cloth if you can.
Never show which one you love.
Go to see each merchant's wares.
Compare and think and breathe in spices:
    hot bite of cayenne,
    fenugreek for *basturma,*
    warm, strong taste of earthy cumin,
    deep red paprika to make a paste,
    crisp allspice for *manti* stuffing,
    mahlap's bitter almond nip.

We buy a bolt of woven wool
tight with pattern and warmth.
Mama says the silks I love
will wait till I'm a wife.

Silks instead of Mama,
silks instead of home.

I search for Vahan in the market,
beside his clocks and chimes.
Arkalian clocks
keep time for miles.
Beirut, Konya, Van.
Baron Bedros, Vahan's father,
works the tiny tools and gears
inside the clocks' bellies.

Vahan paints their faces.
His long-lashed eyes meet mine.
Mama sees and pulls me from him,
back to the Turk to pay,
pinching my hand,
as her voice stays honey sweet.
    "Sosi *jan,* a woman never looks."

Fatima Bey Injeli comes into the stall behind us.
    "Special price for you today,
    gavour, infidel?
    As though you need it,
    already with all the best land."
Mama places the bolt between them.
Her left hip juts out like a ledge.
She stares straight ahead, lips sealed.
The Turk from the shop says to Fatima,
    "The *gavour* are clever with their money,"
as he drops a coin
into Mama's open palm.
    "Teşekkür ederim." Mama thanks him,

nose up, lips drawn tight
like a hard, wrinkled pit.
    "I can buy my cloth from others if you like."
The Turk bows his bald head low,
the fringe of hair around his crown
like an upside-down, bristle-black smile.
    "No, madame. You must come again
    with your lovely daughter.
    The bolt and the price pleased us both."
    "Good day, then," Mama says,
pulling me from the stall,
past the other vendors,
past the crowd,
over the bridge,
squeezing my hand,
muttering,
    "The bee gets honey from the same flower
    where the snake sucks her poison."

She lets go
only when we reach our orchard
spread along the river's edge.
    "I said nothing to that snake
    only because your father
    holds her husband, Mustafa, dear.
    As if I didn't have enough to worry me
    with you making eyes at clockmakers' sons
    before fathers have even spoken?

And Shahen, always wet from the river.
He played with Turkish boys again, you know.
The pair of you will be my end.
And the nerve of that vendor,
insulting us
as we give him good money!
Sosi, look around you.
This is Armenia.
Fat Turks from Constantinople
rule for miles and miles,
making Muslim villagers brazen.
Kurds and Turks may live here too,
but these are our lands.
Your father planted these very vines
with cuttings from my father's arbors
when he was leaving boyhood,
the age of you and Shahen now.
His grandfather's grandfather
planted the olives,
his father,
the apricots.
Nothing came free.
Not the millstones.
Not the earth.
Not the sheep.
Not the wheat.
Generations of sweat.
Don't you ever forget."

Grapevines heavy with fruit
bend over straight wood frames.
Silver olive leaves
shimmer behind them.
Apricots blush in the sun.

Shahen

When she's near me,
Sosi keeps her head bent
to try to spare me shame.
But I know she's taller now.
Everyone knows.

Kevorg used to call us
twin persimmon pits,
Jori and Joreni,
like the two smooth brown seeds
he pulled one day
from the soft, sweet flesh
of a yellow-orange fruit.
Now he's silent.

I'll catch up this fall.
Before the persimmons
ripen again.

At the river,
I'm the smallest.
But water evens us out.
I swim the currents like a fish,
faster than the fastest Turk,

gliding in the waves.
I always win.

My stones skip
far beyond the others.
Bounce, bounce,
ba, ba, ba,
like the beat of a hand on a drum.

But best is when I float.
My weightless body
stretches
from one rocky bank
all
the
way
to
the
other.

Ardziv

I circled above,
watching Shahen
swim in the river
with the young drum caps.

Farther up the river,
a small, fat frog, at water's edge,
caught bugs with his tongue.
A heron soon ate him.
I swooped down and grabbed a fish.
That's when I saw him,
that boy, the drum cap
with the toothy grin.

He was with the man
with the red drum cap
and the stiff white beard
trimmed and combed and polished
so it spread out and down,
like the feathers of a tail.
That man shot my mate.

The instant the bullet hit,
she was gone.

Her flight stopped.
Wings limp, she fell.

The man
clapped the boy
on the shoulders
where wings
would have sprouted
were he a bird.
They laughed.
They watched her fall,
as did I, from our nest,
my talons balled into fists
so as not to harm the chicks.

For forty days,
my mate had stayed there
on the nest
till this brood had hatched,
three eggs this time, with me
bringing all the food
and fresh pine sprigs.

One by one,
the young emerged,
in the order
they were laid,
their egg tooth
breaking

through the shell,
their eyes
partway closed,
no true feathers,
just gray-white down,
and open mouths,
    open shut,
    open shut.

She would never leave them,
in those early days.
It takes two full weeks
for eaglets to hold
their heads up
for feeding.
Open mouths,
    open shut,
    open shut.

She was bigger, swifter,
as are all females of our kind.
But I was good for my size.
That year I brought
so much food
no chick
would need
to eat the other,
so ample
were my hunts.

Young rabbit,
marmot, skunk,
which she shredded
and fed
into their open mouths,
   open shut,
   open shut.

But eagles suffer
when they cannot fly.
As the young
grew strong
and their wings
expanded,
and black-tipped feathers
replaced their down,
the young ones'
appetites peaked.
It was time
for her to fly again.
I pushed her
from the nest
as I had done before.

She flew straight
into a bullet.

The man and boy
ran across the earth

to where she fell,
the man's red hat
bobbing with each step.

They did not
slash her gut
to find sustaining
blood and muscle.
Instead
they plucked her,
starting with her wings,
her glorious wings,
the father
on one side,
the son
on the other.

Each spread
the fingers of one hand
across her skin
to hold it taut
and took feathers
with the other,
one at a time;
taking hold
they snapped their wrists
in one direction
along the axis of its anchor
and then

SNAP
to the opposite side
in an arc
SNAP
to pull it free.

Feather by feather,
they plucked her
naked,
the father's
red hat bobbing
up and down
as he worked, laughing
with his son, rousing
hate inside me for all
the drum-capped ones,
the Turks.

They didn't eat her,
as a hunter would.
They laughed
as she fell
to the ground.

They took her quills,
pulled them from her
and left her naked
for the vultures,

carrion,
a thing we eagles
almost
never
touch.

Mariam ◆ Shahen

Time to play the bird
   game?

Just once.
I have a new game
for us, little bird.
Meg, yergoo, yerek,
one, two, three,

I fly.

to the ground,
where your brother
gives you a stick.

Why?

To learn to write,
Mariam *jan.*

I will be
a writing bird.

Take your stick.
I have mine.
We will write
on the earth.
Father Manoog
says that an angel
showed St. Mesrop
the letters,

wrote them in fire
straight from
God's hand
as St. Mesrop
sat in a cave,
just on that hill
by the church.
But I think he saw
the letters out here.
Look.
Each letter comes
from a shape
in the world.
I'll draw.
You copy.
Three times.
Smaller each time.
Stick is the easiest,
a nice straight line.

Stick, stick, stick.

Then a stick
with a curve
like the head
and the neck
of a swan.

Swan, swan, swan.

And the reflection
of the swan,

35

upside down
in a still pool.

Swan down,
swan down,
swan down.

And a small snake.
Sssssss.

Ssssssnake,
snake, snake.

And a wave, *alik*,
from the wind
on the river.

Alik, alik, alik.

And a step,
astidjan,
like the angels climb
to heaven,
but this time
coming down
to us.

Astidjan,
astidjan,
astidjan.

And a smile, *jbid*,
like the one
on your face,
so big your eyes
disappear.

Smile, smile, smile.

The last two
will be your
favorites.
They too
come from birds.
An oval egg.

Egg.

That's right.
Around to touch
the place you started.

Egg, egg.

And flapping wings.

Flap, flap, flap.
I fly!

These parts make
our letters,
all thirty-eight,
little bird.
What should we write?

Let's write "bird"!
Trchoon,
trchoon,
trchoon!

Trchoon is like this:
stick and wings
make "T."

Stick, wings.

A stick, a swan,
and a wave,
make "R."

"Ch" is stick, stick,
and a smile
to the side.

"Ooh" is two letters.
Stick, snake
and stick, stick.

Stick, swan, wave.

Stick, stick, smile.

Stick, snake.
Stick, stick.

"N" when it is big
starts with wings.
When it is little—

Like me!

yes, like you—
it starts with a smile.
Smile, swan down,
smile.

Smile, swan down,
smile.

Good, little bird.
Good writing.

I am a writing bird.

Sosi

I'm far too young
to wed, I know.
But if Papa would only
speak to Vahan's father,
then we could sit
side by side
at church.

Side by side,
we would touch
the ground in worship,
kiss our own hands,
then forehead,
chest,
left,
right,
and our hands
would rest
on our hearts.

I can see our wedding tree,
almost my size,
with seven slender branches
laden with strings of

apple, pear, and raisin,
their tips joined
through a single *noor*,
a pomegranate fruit,
curled ribbons flowing
from where they meet.

Papa spoke with *baron* Takoushjian,
a man with six daughters,
about a bride for Misak.
Six Armenian daughters
and still he said no,
despite the mill,
despite Misak,
handsome, tall, and strong.

When she heard,
Mama's lips sealed
as tight as a canning jar.
At night I hear her
rasping whisper
saying to Papa,
again and again,
    "I warned you this would happen
    if Anahid married Asan.
    He's a good fine man, as is his father,
    but they are Kurds by blood,
    and we should marry our own."

Shahen

Like water on stone, lessons fall on me.
Again it's St. Mesrop, who sat in a cave,
and the angel who gave him the alphabet.
And back and forth, in time with the clock,
Father Manoog waves his head like a Sunday censer
Through crumbs in his beard, he spits out old stories,
each repetition a black ink inscription proving again
that my fate—*jagadakirus*—written on my forehead,
is not here with priests.
Each book, each map, each history lesson
sends me to my uncle in America.

The chants of yogurt vendors approaching
tell me this school day will finally end.
Turkish calls—
    "*AY-RAN, Ay-ran, ay-ran*"—
change to Armenian—
    "*TAHN, Tahn, tahn*"—
as they near.
But I don't need a cool yogurt drink.
My letter, from my uncle, my *keri*, is my treat.

Dismissed, I run down the mountain path
to my spot in the rocks, open to the river,

hidden from church and from God's prying eyes.
There, in a crack in the stone,
protected from the wind and rain,
one folded paper holds
all of New York Harbor.
The boats, the statue,
the buildings that scrape the sky
like mountaintops come alive
from Keri's letter.
I can see beyond pale pink rocks,
rising above the Euphrates,
all the way to the ocean.

Below me, the great green stripe of river
I will cross to go home
fills with friends and laughter
instead of New York boats.
They're Turks, I know,
but sure, I'll play.
Papa does the same with music.

Sosi   •   Anahid

Anahid *jan*,
my sister bride,
when did you know
that you loved Asan?

Ohhhh, Sosi *jan*!
Are you in love?

No. Not me. No.
I'm too young.
I'm just curious
and I miss you.

Curious.

Yes, curious.

Look at you,
growing up, Sosi *jan*,
though Shahen
seems a little stuck.

I know.

I will tell you.
It came by surprise.
He was always there
every time Papa
had a night of music.
He was like a brother
or a cousin

43

to Misak and Kevorg,
as much as to me.
I was always busy
helping Mama
serve the food.
But one night,
baba Kaban played
a *duduk* melody;
you know how it gets
under your skin
and everything
inside you shimmers?
I looked up and
Asan's eyes met mine.
It was like the *duduk*,
but even stronger.

Whatever the eye sees,
the heart won't forget.

Just a look?

Ardziv

Water and wheel
glistened like gems.
The mill sang its own song,
the low, slow wail
of the wheel as it turned,
the steady pulse
of water on wood,
the rising pitch
as grain became flour,
the rough rock rumble
of the first coarse grind.

It was high summer.
Mounds of apricots
turned one roof golden,
like sun-drenched feather tips.
Shahen and Sosi carried basket
after basket of apricots
from the trees
that lined the river,
Mariam trailing behind them.

I lingered by the river
to study the fruit's

perfect oval shape,
like the velvet pads
on a rabbit's foot.
The seam running up its side
like a cleft between
a lapin nose and mouth,
the indentation
from where stem meets fruit
so like a hollow place
in the soft belly
of a mammal new born.

Once the roof was filled,
Shahen lay back
and stared up
to where I circled
above treetops,
his gaze fixed
on the blue sky.

Shahen   ◆   Sosi

In America, Keri says,
I will go to a school
with hundreds
of students

How could you know
all their names?

I can learn names
by the thousands.

Papa never said
you're going.
And why do you
want to, anyway?
Hundreds of boys,
all the same,
like the apricots
in this heap.
And I've got to pit
every one
while you dream.

Not boys, Sosi.
Young men.
You wait.
I'll climb
to the crown

of Lady Liberty,
the giant statue.
I'll shout
their names
over New York
Harbor.

This one is Adam.
His pit
comes right out.
This one is Eve.
Her pit
comes out, too.
Noah's a bit soft,
overripe.
His pit will stick.

I'll take care
of Noah for you.

Good catch.

Keri says that
from her torch
I will see houses
side by side
spread across
the land
like vines
in an orchard.

Just houses?
No earth?
How will you eat?

Keri says food
comes to the city
by boat and train.

Pah! With food
brought out
from storage
it will be winter
every day.

No, Sosi.
Summer.
Apricot summer,
every day.

Winter
without
you.

Mariam

Bird, *trchoon*.
Stick and wings.
Stick, swan, wave.
Stick, stick, smile.
Stick, snake.
Stick, stick.
Small smile, swan down, smile.

Big smile.
I am a writing bird.

Shahen ◆ *Papa*

Keri was just my age
when he went
to America.

> There were pogroms.
> It made sense, then,
> for him to go,
> though it broke
> your mother's heart.

Papa, pogroms
will come again.

> Where is there a tree
> not shaken
> by the wind?

It makes sense
for me to go.
Keri says
there are free schools
for all the youth
of the city.
If I wait
I'll be too old.

> Leave this land
> where music flows?
> And break again

your mother's heart?
No, Shahen.
And anyway,
you study here
with the priest
already.

Pah!
With Father Manoog,
it's always the same.
Two full years
and I've learned
nothing new.

Shahen,
open your eyes.
Father Manoog
prepares you
for college
in Kharpert.
You're looking
for a donkey
while sitting
on its back.

A donkey!
Exactly, Papa.
Give a donkey
flowers to smell,
and he eats them.
A donkey can swim
seven different strokes,

but the moment
he sees the water,
he forgets them all.
I want more
than donkeys.

You want.
You want.
Always you want.
Stop wanting,
my son,
and then your eyes
will open.

Sosi

Apricots with pierced skin or bruised flesh
boil on a low flame, to make a sweet auburn paste.
Mama stirs them as they thicken.

Juices float from the black pot and perfume the air.
Mama tells me again of the feast
before her brother left for America.

This lets her think of Shahen.
Should he go or should he stay?
The feast is always bittersweet.

Three lambs slaughtered and roasted in a pit,
pilaf rich with pine nuts and dried cherries.
She says she couldn't eat a bite. If it were me, I could,

though Shahen should not go.
If he does, I will write him letters
that make his belly yearn

for the feasts of home.
Mama was already the mother of three
when Keri left. Misak toddling,

Kevorg just brand-new. Anahid five,
like Mariam now. She is scratching again
in the earth with her stick

while Mama tends the black pot's bubbling mixture,
her eye ready for the moment just before it hardens,
so our *bastegh* will stay solid-soft,

like leather,
when spread in thin sheets to dry.
Dusted with ground sugar

and rolled compact,
one December bite
will fill me with summer.

Apricots spread thin on the tray,
an auburn sunset sea.
I pull a strip from the nearest edge,

so thin no one can tell,
and squeeze it
in my palm

into a small, warm ball
that hides inside my cheek
till it melts.

Golden sweetness fills all of me,
like just one glance
from Vahan.

Ardziv

Green mountain fields turned into gold
as wheatgrass curled and ripened.
Harvest songs rose from the fields
as sickles slashed the stalks.
The Kurdish *beys* took in their tithe.
The peasants kept the rest.
Turks and Kurds hauled in their crops
and left the mill with haste.
They would not chat
with those whom they called *gavour*s.
Armenian farmers lingered.

Hot summer nights, the roof became
the summer dining room.
Mountain winds swept away
the heat of the day
and music filled the air.
Papa hobbled up the stairs,
his left leg dragged behind.
But both his hands,
they worked just right,
pressing the neck,
plucking the strings,

the quill tip tucked
between thumb and first finger,
the plume end flowing
out from under
his curved palm.

One August dusk, as the sun hung low
and colors filled the sky,
Mama and Sosi spread a rich red cloth
across the roof floor,
with platters of food upon the cloth:
rice wrapped tight with leaves from grapevines,
cheese fibers pulled so thin they might line a nest,
flat baked bread from fresh-ground wheat,
the black pot filled with green-pepper *dolma*,
apricots, olives, and skewers of lamb,
juice of the meat still running red.
Misak and Kevorg
splashed in the stream
to clear their hair of wheat dust.
Shahen carried Mariam
on his shoulders,
holding her round knees
as he darted down the path
to greet the guests.

Mariam flapped her arms
above him

like a baby bird,
unbending her knees
and rising
at the sight of Anahid,
who quickened her step
when she saw them.
I flew in quite close,
not believing my eyes
at the sight of her husband
and his parents, behind her.
They wore head scarves
and prayer shawls.
This was a family of Kurds!

Kurds who pray with the drum caps,
bowing south five times each day.
Young Asan, the husband of Anahid,
his parents, Kaban and Palewan.

In his arms Kaban carried
two pipe instruments:
a long, straight *duduk*
and a *zurna*
with a bell at its base,
both made from the wood
of an apricot tree,
hollowed and holed,
blown through double reeds.
I've heard them both before.

The *zurna*'s reed
is a thin wheat leaf
rolled tight.
Its sound pierces the air.
But the *duduk,*
with its flat, loose reed,
makes a sad, sweet sound,
like a call to a loved one
about to take flight
to a distant land.

Shahen set Mariam down on the ground.
He kissed each guest
in turn on both cheeks.
Palewan placed a fine plate of sweets
in his hands, twenty tiny nests,
four by five, in neat rows,
made of fine-cut dough
filled with ground green nuts
swimming in sticky syrup.
　　"*Digin* Palewan," Shahen said.
　　"I dream about your *kadayif.*"
　　"There's no *kadayif* like this in America,
I'm sure," she replied.
　　"Then I will have to eat my dreams when I go."
Back toward the house, Mariam walked
and then flew, suspended
between the hands of Anahid and Palewan.

Such hugging and laughter
up on the roof, sharing the meal
like one family.
Imagine!
Kurds and Armenians together,
as if falcons and eagles
had just become one.

Last light faded
from the sky as they ate,
but surprises did not end.
Another lone man
came up the path,
with a curious slanted walk.
He pressed and pushed to arrive,
leading with his heart,
a *dumbek* drum, its sides inlaid
with mother-of-pearl,
held tight against his body.
His arm squeezed the drum's waist,
the goatskin taut
across its top.
But something pulled him
from the backs of his legs
as he moved forward.
A round drum cap
on his head said
no mistaking it:
this Mustafa

was a Turk!
Imagine!
Like falcons and hawks
right inside my nest.

It was one of them,
a falcon or a hawk,
it had to have been,
who came to my nest
after the drum cap
shot my mate.
Tucked into rock
high on a ledge,
the nest could be reached
only by one with wings.
I had left them alone,
the young ones.
I had no choice.
Their mouths
were always open,
   open shut,
   open shut,
their flight feathers
not yet full.
I had waited in the nest
till I spied
a plump gray rabbit.
Within minutes
I was back,

my beak full
of flesh
for them.
But the nest
was already
empty.

Hidden by night now,
I dropped down
to low branches
as the music began.
Soothing music,
music soothing my sore heart.
My quill plucked
sweet sounds
from the strings
of the *oud,*
drawing me in.
Shahen too.

Mustafa's steady hand
beat his *dumbek.*
Kaban's cheeks
emptied, then filled,
the *duduk* sound unceasing
with his constant breath.

Lydian melodies like oil flowed.
Mother tongues in unison blending

thick umber of Turkish coffee,
Armenian apricots, ginger ripe,
blue Kurdish moonlight above us.

Misak and Kevorg stood
arms out, hands on shoulders,
catching the beat of the song,
the *tamzara*, with their step.
One—two—three,
stomp, stomp.
One—two—three,
stomp, stomp.
Asan joined the line, now an arc,
Mama and Palewan, between them.
One—two—three,
stomp, stomp.

Shahen did not dance.
He had eyes only for my quill.
His lips turned up
as Papa pulled
my quill across the string.

But as the song ended,
Shahen jumped up.
Sosi, too.
They pulled Anahid
to her feet

to make her dance
with Asan next.
The young couple
wound around each other
like eagles courting,
though one of them had falcon blood,
talons locked,
cartwheeling through the sky,
the line between their eyes never breaking.
The melody of the slow, sweet song
twisted and turned around itself,
our eyes all on them:
Mustafa, tender and sweet,
Kaban and Papa proud,
Misak and Kevorg dreaming.
Mothers blushed.
Children shushed.

Sounds of the stream
on the stone
and the wood
filled the air,
till Papa rose to stand,
his hand across his heart.
    "My wife's brother is a faraway fool
    to hold back his blessing for Anahid and Asan.
    Here it is clear. You men are my brothers.
    Our holy books differ by one prophet only.

"The sun does not shine
on one man and his family
keeping others in the dark,
even in New York."

When falcons or hawks came to my nest,
I must confess, I sang a different song.

Shahen

Papa always played,
but I did not hear
the *oud* before,
not like this.

Long, deep notes
pull me up to the sky.
The plucks of the quill
dance on my spine.

But best of all,
if I learn to play,
Papa will have to
let me go,

because then,
someone
will play *oud*
in America.

Sosi

After their dance,
I had to tell her.
I whispered it.
I poured Vahan
right into
Anahid's ear,
his glances at the market,
a seat nearby at church,
while Papa and his friends
played into the night.

Soon we will sit
side by side.
My secret's safe with her.

Ardziv

By noon the next day
I found Mustafa in the village.
A drummer with a drum cap,
a fine, tall house,
and a hard, bitter wife.
Fatima.

On the rooftop, shelling pistachios with another,
she opened her hollow red lips to speak.
I saw past her tongue, her teeth, and her throat,
to deep in her belly,
where she hungered
for finer clothes,
more things,
their land.
    "Mustafa made music
    again with Kaban
    and the Armenian.
    I tell him do not go there.
    It breaks my father's heart.
    I tell him,
    but his ears stay closed as unripe nuts.
    The *gavour*s have all the best land.
    They hire Turkish boys to watch their sheep

so their pretty son can study with priests.
They charge me more
to grind wheat.
I know it.
Other *gavour*s pay less,
I'm sure.
And the carpets,
how can they have such carpets
on a miller's wages
unless they are taking from us?"
A bitter taste came up from my crop.
Not fear. Eagles never fear.
Mustafa, a man of steady, sweet beat,
lived with this Fatima,
who gnawed on the world like a third lamb
masticating its mother's udder
to make a fresh hole for the milk
when siblings have hold of the teats.

I hunt these ones first.

Shahen

Stuck in a front-row pew
thick with incense.
Father Manoog slips into his sermon trance.
Bleating sheep sounds blend with his chants.
The voices of my friends, at the river,
free from Sunday service,
penetrate the thick stone walls.
I'm stuck here with pictures,
the same old pictures
painted life-sized
on the wall.

Noah's Ark
catching hold
of Mount Ararat.
First the raven,
then the dove
that flew above
receding waters
and found the
olive branch.

And Joseph
forgiving his brothers

for selling him into slavery.
Pah! I would punch
Misak and Kevorg
smack in the nose
if they did such a thing to me.

One focused beam of light
from the tiny dome-top window
pours into this dark stone church.

If I were a rock
I'd hurl myself through that window.
But I wouldn't stop
plunk
at the river to play.
I would fly
over my friends
through the sky
to New York.

Mariam ◆ *Sosi*

Look, a bird!

> Shhhh.
> Quiet in church.

Through the window.

> Shhhh.

Up. Look!

> Shhhh.

Please?

> Oh!
> An eagle.

Ardziv.

> Like the one
> who gave us
> Shahen's quill.

Yes.

> Vahan turns
> his head,
> not to me,
> not in church,
> but up,
> to the eagle.

See?

> Shhhh.
> Yes.

72

With her little
fingertip
Mariam draws
letters on my leg,
sending shivers
up my spine,
just like
one look
from Vahan.

Ardziv

From the church I rose skyward
over pink dry mountaintops,
looking for plump rabbit, squirrel,
or snake sunning himself
against the coming cold,
lying in wait
for a lizard or a rat.

A slender whip snake,
dusky red,
made its way
to a young warbler
picking bugs
from a crack in the stone.
Before the snake struck
I swooped
and grabbed its
head and neck
between my talons.
It turned spirals
as I flew
and I squeezed
till it stopped
and I pushed

the coiled snake
into my crop.

My belly full,
the winds calm,
I found the house of Kaban.
Side by side
at the rooftop loom,
Palewan and Anahid
worked the wool.
The *kilim*'s pattern,
Kurdish, of course,
of interlocking diamonds.

Rust, rose, and red,
blue, brown, and beige.
I never noticed before
how inside of
each diamond
is a cross.

Sosi

Anahid comes from the market
filled with stories of the season's first figs,
clock chimes, and news of the new Balkan war.
The Ottoman Turks will lose more land.

Mama listens, her wooden spoon
swirling the milk inside the black pot.
Mama reminds us,
as though we have never made yogurt before,
    "To make *madzoon,*
      you must move the milk
      when it's over the heat
      so it doesn't curdle.
      Bring it almost to a boil.
      No further."
Around in circles Mama stirs the milk,
till a vapor almost starts to rise.
Then she moves the black pot
from the fire, her back to us.
As she scrapes the remains
of the last *madzoon* batch
into the pot's pure white milk,
Anahid slips me
a folded piece of paper.

I open it to see
Sayat Nova's poem,
in Vahan's fluid hand,
his letters lovely loops and lines:
"I beheld my love this morning."
I tuck the paper in my pocket
so Mama doesn't see.
I let his words echo
as Mama continues.

    "Seeds live inside
    what came before.
    This is a very good culture.
    I've never let it die,
    not since my mother
    gave it to me
    when I first married.
    You must heat the milk first
    so only *madzoon* seeds will grow
    in the fresh, clean milk."

Mariam

Grapes ripe
and blessed,
we pick.
I eat.
Pop, sweet.
Spit out pits.

Hampers,
cutters,
baskets lined
with sheets.
Pop, sweet.
Spit out pits.

No milling for three days
as my brothers
load our donkeys
and others help us pick
and sing and pick.
My brothers walk
the donkeys home
and come back

for more bunches,
sweet and round,

white and red,
till the sun goes down
and we lie on our carpets
next to the vines
as the stars appear.

Papa plays us to sleep
by the vines. I dream.
We pick.
I eat.
Pop, sweet.
Spit out pits.

Ardziv

As olives turned
from green to black
and warbler's second brood
hatched and fledged, I watched.

Shahen showed Mariam
new words for her stick.
Each day she scratched
long lines of letters
into the earth,
leading like paths
in rings around the mill.
She wrote his name.

Shahen.
    Wave and smile to the side.
    Smile, smile, half smile.
    Stick, small snake.
    Swan down, half smile, stick.
    Smile, swan down, smile.
Shahen.

In distant lands
lines of soldiers

moved locust-like
across the earth,
their bodies clad
in identical
greens and browns,
rifles up like antennae.

Sosi

A letter came today from our *keri*.
Mama breathes in memories of her brother.
She tucks the sealed envelope into her dress,
where it waits for Papa and my brothers
to join us on the rooftop for lunch.

Millstones grind to stopping.
Papa, Misak, and Kevorg
brush wheat dust from their clothes.
They splash their hands and faces clean.

I tie tight knots of deep red wool
into the pattern growing on my loom.
Shahen tosses Mariam into the sky.
His rhythm, his chant, taking all the air.

A-me-ri-ca,
A-me-ri-ca,
A-me-ri-ca.

When Papa, Misak, and Kevorg sit,
Shahen puts Mariam into my lap.
Mama kisses the letter, hands it back to Papa.
Our twelve eyes rest on him as he reads Keri's words.

"War has come.
You must go.
You are Christians alone
in the Ottoman center.
At least send Shahen."
Mama draws a short sharp breath.
Papa's brow makes one thick line.
Shahen wears a jackal's grin.

"In America, sons grow tall
like plane trees.
Armen, still in school,
already towers over me.
He speaks English like a prince.
Shahen will do the same here."
Mama's face turns to ash.
Shahen's teeth show through his smile.

"See, Papa. It's good I should go."
Water hits the wooden wheel
like the steady beat of a drum.

"There is no reason for war
that reasonable men can't solve."
Papa's words like a melody
blend with the mill stream
till Mama stops the song.

"But can we trust them to be reasonable?"
Papa says,

"I decide who comes and goes.
Your brother is too far to know."
Papa's voice is like rough rock.

Shahen swallows back his grin,
but I see his eyes are dancing.

The water on the mill wheel
makes a constant beat.
Calm comes to Papa's face.
    "There is no *them,*
    only single souls.
    Mustafa.
    Kaban.
    They would never harm us.
    This is our home."

Shahen's eyes go to the sky,
his lips pressed tight,
his twisted smile rising.
Inside my ears, I buzz and burn.
Every day with Father Manoog
and still Shahen does not know
that the stones of home
are the warmest.

Shahen ♦ Mariam

One, two, three,

into a cloud
with a beautiful
house full of rain.

You watch
from above
till the flowers
in the fields
are thirsty.

Then you open
your windows
and let the rain
fall to the ground.
Splash!

Meg, yergoo, yerek,

into a cloud
that blows

I fly

A rain house.

Choor door.
Give me water.

Again!

I fly

across the sea
to a land
where brothers
speak like princes
and grow very tall.

Sosi

With Mama and Mariam
and the morning sun,
I go to put the vines to sleep.

It takes us five full days
to do the twenty rows
of our twenty-*baran* vineyard.

We collect the staves.
We bring the vines together,
lay them on the ground,

cover them with soil
with stones on top
to secure them.

Shahen

Papa tells me that the secret of the sound
is in the right hand
and the pick,
the *mizrap*.

Papa tells me that mystery and power
come in through the quill,
that eagles were with us
long before Christ.

Papa tells me to hold it light and loose
between my fingertips, hand and wrist fluid,
like bubbling water, to let the supple quill pull
music from each pair of strings.

Again, Papa tells me a good Armenian carries
the music of home close to his heart, wherever he is.
If he lets me go,
I will.

Papa tells me to let the *oud* belly touch my own,
to tuck its side into my right elbow, its neck resting
in my left hand, two melon bellies touching,
yes.

Papa tells me to make my left hand fierce.
Fingers like hammers
press into metal
for song.

Papa tells me it only hurts at first.
Calluses will form with time.
Then my fingers will dance on the strings,
the way my brothers danced across the rooftop

before the Ottomans entered the war,
fighting with Germany,
against Russia, England,
and France.

Papa does not tell me that the Turks blame us,
the Christians, as their Empire rots and shrinks.
All this I learned
for myself.

Sosi

Mama and I worked the dough
with sweet fresh flour from the mill.
Anahid brought news today
not of war,
not of Vahan,

though the news was for me,
only me.
She whispered it,
poured it right into my ear
while Mama worked the *tonir*,
dropping sheets of dough
onto the clay surface
of the underground oven
she had built.

I kept my face as still as glass.
Her secret's safe with me.

She's not sure,
not completely.
Thunder clouds don't always give rain,
you know.
But I know.

Her rosy lips and cheeks know, too.
They are proof that next spring,
after the pink buds of apricots
burst into bloom,
after the small, hard fruits first form,
and then blush sweet and ripe,
their scent spreading
through the whole valley,

I will be an auntie.

Shahen

Fall persimmons ripened,
but I stayed small.

Cold came down from mountaintops.
Still I have not grown.

Young Turks will fight the Russian troops
and still my face is smooth.

Armenian men will join the Turks;
so say the new laws.

Troops prepare for eastern fronts
at Erzerum so near.

But Papa only plays the *oud*.
I say to him after a song,

"Turkish guns will turn on us.
You must let me go.

"Misak and Kevorg too.
Soon they'll be the age to serve."

The *oud* between us,
my callused fingers tough,

my voice too high,
my face too like a girl's.

Papa will not listen.

Sosi

I meet Anahid at the market.
No belly bulge of baby
shows below her coat.
But I know.
    "Let's shop for a clock,"
she says, eyes bright,
her lips and cheeks
pomegranate-red.

She tells *baron* Arkalian
the clock will be a present
for her husband's mother, Palewan.
He stiffens ever so slightly
at this mention of a Kurd,
but a master craftsman
shows his wares to all.

He shows Anahid
the fine details
of painted faces,
the inner workings
of the gears,
and the glistening polish
of the wooden frame.

From across the shop,
Vahan looks to me.
Baron Arkalian brings us
to Vahan's bench
to show us the finest brushes,
made from three cat whiskers
aligned just so they can make
a tapering line.

Vahan is so close
that my skin shimmers
as though the brush
makes lines on me.

Ardziv

Cold came. Leaves fell.
Snakes stayed in caves
for their winter sleep.
No one worked on rooftops.
Each day my search
for beast or bird
took me far
from the music
of home.

Winter days,
as I rose higher,
I saw soldiers
by the thousands
climbing snow-clad slopes
and forging cold mud valleys,
swarming the rocks
like an angry herd.
Identical *kabalak* helmets
made their heads
look swollen,
like beasts
instead of
humans.

From farther east,
train cars filled with soldiers,
clad in coats like bears,
landed at a fort
and began to fight the others.

One day, as I looked back toward home,
I caught a glimpse of Shahen
descending toward the river.
I flapped and soared,
helped by the wind
to arrive at the river's edge,
where a group of boys, almost men,
the same ones he swam with in summer,
including the one with the toothy grin,
called him traitor as he passed.
    "Go to Russia!
    That's where you belong,
    greedy Christian traitor!"
Shahen did not shrink or hide.
He stood as tall as he could
with his small size,
his voice still high like Sosi's.
    "I will leave you all
    in the dust
    when I go
    to America."

II
MASSACRE
1915

Sosi

Long, cold months,
I work at the loom inside,
with Vahan's note tucked under the loom
so its words flow through me as I weave.
"Like the nightingale, I warbled round my rose
with wings displayed."

Five hands more
will make this carpet done,
this carpet for my dowry,
with colors from my heart,
though our fathers haven't spoken
not with the war, not with Vahan
almost old enough to serve.
Misak, too, who was foolish enough
to cheer when the law was changed
so Armenians could serve
in the Ottoman army.

Inside the pattern of diamonds and leaves,
I've knotted birds into full fearless flight.
Others perch on branches, feet clasping tight.
One lies still, in her neat rush nest,
three blue eggs below her warm body.

She's plump, this bird, like Anahid,
with a calm and glowing full-moon face.
I made her here, smiling with me,
not scared of those who'd turn on her
because she's one of us.
For now she must be nothing but
the good pregnant wife
of a Kurdish soldier.

I start a new bird who dreams as he sleeps.
He lies on his side, eyes closed, his red chest tucked
between a blanket of wings, his beak tilted up.
My knots make him seem more dead than dreaming.
Perhaps birds dream only when they fly.
Mama forbids me to take out the rows.
It wastes good wool, she says,
and mistakes make the next carpet better.

But I take out each knot
with a small knife
hiding the fistful of
rich red wool
deep in my pocket.
"Take the knife and slay me straight away,"
says the poet Sayat Nova.

Mama will never know.

Shahen

On frosty nights, paperlike sheets of ice
form where stones
block the stream's flow.
I pry them up, the icy shapes,
so like states on maps,
and shatter them on the rock.
Morning music for my walk
to Father Manoog.

Our stream flows strong
from winter snow and rain.
Its rushing sound fills my ears
and blocks the steps of soldiers,
four of them, who appear on the banks
pointing their guns, saying,
    "You, boy. Take me to the *gavour* miller."
I obey, knowing Papa and my brothers
are already at work.
Soldiers storm inside, shouting,
    "Surrender your arms!"
Misak stops the millstones.
Kevorg steps back against the wall.
Papa takes one step toward them,
his arms out at chest height, palms up,

as though he is in church.

"What arms?" Papa asks them.

"We millers have no need for arms."
Gentle Papa opens every door and chest,
hiding nothing but his limp.
Soldiers dump out bins of clean white flour
and whole wheat berries onto the earthen floor.
They rake it with their guns.

"We millers have no need for arms,"
Papa says as they poke him
toward the door of our attached house.
They tear Mama's blankets.
They take our copper bowls.
They dump her food from pots and jars
and tell us, "We will be back tomorrow.

If you do not give us your weapons then,
limp and all, we will arrest you."

After they leave, Papa sends me to Mustafa
for a weapon to surrender in the morning.
We millers have a need for weapons.

Sosi

Armenians of the age to serve
now build the Baghdad Railway.
One straight Turkish German line
from Constantinople
to the oil fields of Basra.

From paintbrush
to sledgehammer,
this cannot be for Vahan.
Or my brothers, either,
though Shahen's far too small to serve.

The Ottomans sent Asan
to fight at the Russian front.
But other Kurds,
the thieves released from jails,
join roving bands called *chetes*.

Ardziv

Before the days
became longer than nights,
everywhere I flew
there was war.

Sharklike ships
burned through
the Black Sea.
The Mediterranean

and the Red,
the same.
Fires blazed in the Suez.
Ships left the ocean

to enter the wide, sandy mouth
of the Euphrates,
laying anchor by smokestacks
of Persian oil fields.

The earth itself
seemed to fear.
Bulbs kept hidden
under the earth.

Sheep were late
with lambs.
Ground squirrels
stayed in dens.

But then the days got longer.
Brave apricots pushed out their blooms.
Rooftop life began again.
The mill wheel still made music.

Sosi

Last fall we stoned the vineyard,
our twenty-*baran* vineyard,
twenty lines of vines
safe from winter cold,
covered with earth,
sprinkled with stones,
as if to mark a grave.

I pull aside the stones
and dig into the soft earth
to find the rough brown vines.
Slight swells,
red buds
dot their skin.
I bring them
into the April light
that warms my face

but cannot reach
our leaders,
who sit in prison cells.
They search our home
for guns again.

This time they smash
the porcelain pots
from Abder village
that Palewan
gave to Mama.

Shahen

Sunday services shrink, not in length.
Each week, we are fewer.
The censer still swings back and forth.
Holy Fathers and deacons
still chant every word
in this church built on the ground
where the angels came
with the alphabet
so we could write to God.
But when Father Manoog
gets to reading scriptures,
the "blessed peacemakers" are gone.
Instead he reads of war,
   "nation rising against nation,
    and kingdom against kingdom,"
and I think of Papa,
who says there is no them,
no other nations,
no other kingdoms,
and I know he is wrong.

Seventy men
from Havav village

now sit in Palu prison
with leaders from the town.
Some families leave or hide,
goodbye whispers
part of church.
I pray to Papa,
not to God,
to let us go, too.
He's the one
who dreams of peace,
that friendships
will protect us.
It's his eyes, not mine,
that must open
before the soldiers
come again.

A tangle of men outside the church
waits for Father Manoog in the bright light.
Baron Arkalian steps forward,
Beirut bound, his family at his heels.

Vahan, his eldest,
looks toward the women
waiting under walnut trees,
their barely budding branches
spread like black veins
against the blue sky.

Only one of them
stares back
at the men:
Sosi,
her body
newly curved.

I try to catch her eye
to make her stop.
But she sees only Vahan.
His father asks for
more than farewell blessings.
He wants us all to leave.
He knows the time.

Sosi takes a step toward them.
But Mama's hands
catch both her shoulders,
turning Sosi, like a wheel,
back toward home.

Before Father Manoog can speak,
Papa says,
        "Bedros, you are mistaken.
        This sacred earth has been ours
        for generations. Turks here,
        they know this.
        They know us.
        This will protect us."

But Father Manoog makes
the sign of the cross
over *baron* Bedros,
his wife, and his children.
Vahan's head is now bowed low.
    "Go in peace," he tells them.
    "May peace be with you on your journey."
Father Manoog makes the sign of the cross
over the crowd
closing in around him.
Papa stands back,
his neck hard,
like rocks and a chain.
But his voice booms
back into the crowd,
    "If we leave these mountains,
    they will never be ours again.
    We must trust our friends.
    The voice of the people is louder
    than the boom of a cannon."

Sosi

Mama's hands dig into my shoulders
as she pushes me toward home.
    "Shame on you, Sosi,"
    she says with each step.
He'll come back,
I know it.
He'll come back
to find me.
When the trouble passes,
he'll come back home.
Let them think he left me
like a sack of wheat.
But I know the truth.
He'll come back
to find me.
I will never leave.
    "Shame on you, Sosi.
    Shame on you," she says
as we step through the door to our home.
She pushes me right to loom.
    "I should not have let you keep that poem.
    It gave you an empty promise.
    Fathers decide all in this life.
    This you must know.

Now give it to me.
We will turn it to ash."
Mama pushes
the top of the loom
into the wall.
Its base rises enough
for my fingertips to grasp
the folded paper.
I don't have to read it again.
I know the words by heart.
I know each curve
of Vahan's hand.
Mama takes it and touches
paper to ember.
Smoke rises toward the black pot
suspended above the fire,
dolma made with last year's grape leaves
simmering inside it.
I squeeze the red wool
deep in my pocket.

Mariam

When all of us
have gone to bed,
Papa and Mama
fight and fight.

I put
one ear
on Sosi's
shoulder,
my fist
inside
the other.
Sosi says,
      "*Os, os, os,*
      it's all right.
      All right.
      All right."

Sosi

Mama says that fathers decide all.
But each night she makes her case with Papa.
If soldiers come again,
Papa's friends can do nothing.
She says Papa mistakes
*maqam*s of music
for bonds among men.
She says Mustafa Bey Injeli
cannot even control his wife.
Mama says, imagine, him a butcher,
the one with the sharpest knives in town,
and he cannot stop his wife?

It's true.
Already old Fatima wears kerchiefs
edged in lace, like Anahid's,
with the pattern of a new bride
now almost a mother.
Fatima stole them
from boarded-shut homes.
She struts proud like a girl rooster.
Her husband feels shame.

Papa says carpets
fray at the edges,
not at the center,
where the weave is tight.

It's true
about carpets.
It takes a knife
to cut the center.

I squeeze
the red wool
deep
inside
my pocket.
Then I stroke
Mariam's
soft black curls
till she finds
the depth of sleep.

The sound of water
hitting stone
echoes through
the night.
Sleep, come to me.
Vahan, come to me.
I'll meet you

in my dreams.
Anoush koonuh,
sweet sleep,
please come.

Ardziv

Each day the young ones
walk to the vines by the river,
the vines that face to the east
to catch the rising sun.
Shahen carries the staves.
Sosi carries string
and a pruning knife.
Mariam picks May flowers.

Shahen leaves the staves
and crosses the bridge
for his lessons.
Sosi prunes the vines
so one strong shoot remains,
which she ties to the stave
so the grapes will hang down.
Mariam picks May flowers.

Shahen

Papa says we are safe.
We have lived with Kurds and Turks
for generations.

Papa says we are safe.
Some families packed everything and went east
for refuge in higher mountains.

Papa says mountains hold dangers of their own.
Some families head to Constantinople
to catch boats to America or France.

Papa says they are fools. The Balkan front
will just trap them in Constantinople.
Some head south to live with the Arabs.

Papa says there are too many risks.
The Ottomans rule most Arab lands too.
Pogroms will not come to Palu.

Papa says we are brave.
Other Armenians act like prisoners,
losing honor inside their own homes.

Papa tells me other boys dress as girls.
I picture them, the Kacherian boys,
in dresses over trousers,

scarves wrapped round their heads.
I wonder
were their ears pierced too?

I ask him, "When can I go to America?"
Like water flowing through stones in the stream,
his answer shifts to find a new path.

"After the trouble passes,"
Papa tells me.
Palu will be safe.

Sosi

Soldiers come with guns
straight to the mill room door.
They shout until the grinding stops
and Papa, Misak, and Kevorg come out.

Soldiers point and poke with their guns.
They take my brothers,
Kevorg and Misak,
their hands tied together,

Shahen safe at school.
They pull Mama from my brothers,
Kevorg and Misak,
their hands tied together.

Mariam stays away
with her stick, watching,
as they take our brothers,
hands tied.

Papa tries to stop them.
But they tie their hands,
Misak and Kevorg.
They point and poke with their guns.

They say it's for their safety,
for all the young men,
all the ones with bristles.
They would have taken Vahan

for his safety, too.
But he's gone,
thanks be to God.
I know he'll come back.

They tied their hands
and they point and poke their guns
at Kevorg and Misak, taken
with their hands tied.

Baron Kaban
comes to our home.
He stands beside Papa
in his Muslim prayer shawl.

He tells them
Papa's honest,
not a revolutionary.
He tells them

our family has
three daughters
and two sons at home.
But we are two daughters,

only two.
Anahid is not with us.
Only two.
Baron Mustafa arrives.

He says the same.
Soldiers believe them.
Why would Muslims
lie for *gavour*s?

Kevorg and Misak,
taken,
my two brothers,
their hands tied.

Mustafa and Kaban
leave when the soldiers do.
It would seem wrong
for them to stay with us.

Mama holds me and Mariam close.
We pray for Shahen,
safe at school,
Kevorg and Misak taken.

We pray the Turkish soldiers
didn't go there first.
They point and poke with their guns
but they do not shoot.

The next hours, we stay on the roof,
watching for Shahen.
We almost don't breathe.
Our eyes on the path,

Papa pacing.
Kevorg and Misak taken,
their hands tied,
imagining Shahen home.

Mariam's silent.
Her eyes on the path.
Scratching the roof with her stick,
imagining Shahen home.

Mama makes me hem a new kerchief.
She makes me embroider its edges
with the pattern of an unwed girl.
My eyes stick to the path,

imagining Shahen home,
Vahan home.
Papa pacing.
Kevorg and Misak taken.

With each stitch
the needle stabs
my fingertip.
Blood spots stain

the white cloth red,
like the forbidden wool
deep in my pocket
that I cut

from the carpet
because the bird
looked dead.
Misak and Kevorg taken.

Mama sews too, her hands
like a hummingbird's wings,
taking in one of her dresses.
Their hands tied.

Our eyes stick to the path,
imagining Shahen home.
Papa pacing.
Kevorg and Misak taken, hands tied.

We are ready when Shahen comes,
not down the path's center
but behind one tree to another,
not taken,

almost silent,
till his sounds and steps
burst open
when he sees Mama

running
with a small bundle of her work
clutched to her side,
Papa two steps behind her.

I hold Mariam tight.
I keep watch from the roof.
They smother him with kisses.
They pull him inside.

My eyes on the empty path.
Flapping clothes surround us,
hanging in weak gray light.
Kevorg and Misak taken,

hands tied together.
Inside my parents speak
and speak
and dress him.

At dusk
they introduce him
to us,
our sister.

Shahandukht.

Mariam

Where's Misak?
Where's Kevorg?
Why did soldiers take them?
Where are they?
Mama says they're
with the soldiers
working for the army,
the bad soldiers
with teeth like dogs
and pointed guns
who tied their hands,
and all day
Mama cries
and sews
and cries
and sews.

Shahen wears her dress.

Shahen

Papa so thick,
so certain,
so simple.
He lost three sons
in one day:
my brothers
to soldiers,
and me
to a scarf and dress.

Mama knows my shame.
Still, she shows me
women's tricks,
like how to pull
a new dark hair,
if one should grow
on my chin or lip,
out from the root
by the nails
of my thumb
and finger.
    "To shave
    would make it
    thicken,"

she tells me,
though she knows
I have no need.

My brothers will return someday,
standing tall like men
with full black beards.

They must.

Ardziv

I followed the soldiers
with every fit
Armenian man.
Papa spared
because his limp
would slow him.
They walked them
in a line
along the river
for miles,
pushing
and poking
with guns,
their hands tied.
They stopped.
They stripped them.
They turned them.
They shot them.
They threw the bodies
into the river.

Bodies washed up and lodged
between stones
on the river's edge.

Vultures swooped down
to eat them.
I've taken carrion
from vultures before.
Sometimes eagles do this.
But that day I flew off.
I found a goat
away from his herd,
tore his muscles to pieces
with my beak and talons
until I could eat no more.
I flew upriver
and left the carcass behind.

Shahen

My brothers are gone, taken.
As a child, I was spared.
The soldiers came to school that day.
They looked at all our faces.
They took anyone with bristles
and left the baby-faced behind.
They argued about some of us.
But my case was clear.
In their eyes,
I was too young to fight.

Then Father Manoog told us,
the baby-faced,
to hide in the cliffs
behind the old fort
till the sun was low,
and like a child, I obeyed.
Then I crossed the bridge
to home.

I want to fight the Turkish soldiers.
I want to work the mill.
    "No," Papa tells me.
    "To keep you safe

dressed as you are
you must do women's work.
I will work the mill alone,
what little work there is,
till harvest next comes in.
By the end of a year,
this trouble will pass."

He speaks fine,
but he cannot look at me.
And Mama sews like a machine.
Mariam asks for Kevorg and Misak
while Sosi and I chop bitter onions.

We eat food brought out from storage.
Cabbage leaves with black age spots,
withered beets and carrots,
cracked wheat retrieved
from the mill room floor
and the soldiers' raking guns.
Mama and Sosi still bake bread.
Our hens lay eggs.
Kaban sends one goat each week
from Kurdish mountain herds.
We do not roam
the woods for greens.
We have mint
that grows by the stream.
We do not go to market.

By the end of a year, I will grow
and I'll show Papa
that I'm the man he's not.
He lacks the courage to leave here.
For him all life is like a song,
with different voices blending.

Now Mama embroiders
more kerchiefs
for me.

Sosi, her lips and cheeks like berries,
hides when soldiers come.
One soldier pokes my skirt with his gun.
He eyes my flat chest,
proof to him that I'm pure.
Proof to me that Papa's an old hen
hovering till the soldier is gone.

I can act.
Like a letter,
I will go to America.

Sosi ◆ Shahen

Come tie with me,
Shahen *jan*.
The work is good.
The knots' colors
down each row
add up to make
the pattern.
Pass the weft
with this shuttle
to bind the edges,
then beat it
with the comb.
Pack the fibers tight.
Will you try?

                                        Sosig, I can't.

Come on, Shahen.
Time will pass
as we tie. First,
a few red knots
for the edge. Next,
the bird's blue belly.
Take the end
of the thread
and go over

one warp thread,
then under the next
and back to
where I start,
then snip.
You try.

This is your work.
Not mine.

Come on, Shahen.
The loom will hide you.
Come tie this knot.
Here, I tied it.
Will you cut the end?

Don't give me a knife.

I'll finish the bird.
Anahid and I
would race
to the middle.

You'll win.

We're not racing.
Just tie.

My fingers cannot
do such things.

Last summer seems
so far away.
Anahid's baby
will be coming soon.

Think of something
else to say!

138

That's women's talk.
I'm not Mama
or *digin* Palewan,
about to be a
grandmother.

I miss the music,
don't you?

Not one bit.
We'd all have left
if Papa wasn't
fooled by music.

At least you
must miss
Anahid.

Yes.
Misak and
Kevorg too.

This carpet
full of birds
will be yours.
You can take it
to America.

I'll never go now.

You will.
You'll see.
You'll go soon.
Take the red now.
For the background.
That's right.

Over, under,
back, and tie.
Snip.
Over, under,
back, and tie.
Over, under,
back, and tie.

                                        Snip.

Over, under,
back, and tie.

Ardziv

Soldiers were close again.
I flew tight circles around the mill.
Papa stood outside looking up,
shaking his head.
I hovered in the air above him
as he reached both hands
into the sky,
spread his five fingers
toward me,
through me,
palms up,
open to the sky.
    "Forgive me.
    I was wrong.
    I fear my sons are dead.
    Their spirits come to me
    each night.
    No land is worth
    a child's life.
    Protect them.
    Please.
    The ones who still live."
Then he drew his palms
back into fists,

his eyes still high in the sky,
looking through me,
and he pulled these fists
down to his gut.

I landed on a lower branch,
a silent witness.
He raised his arms to the sky again,
opened his palms,
then pulled both open hands
down to his heart.
Then he touched the ground
with his right hand,
kissed the back of his hand,
then forehead,
chest,
left,
right,
and let his hand rest
on his heart,
his eyes and mouth
squeezed shut,
taking no breath
for one long minute.

He swallowed.
Breath came again.
His eyes opened
and met mine.

142

He shivered.
He bowed
his head
to his chest
and went
inside.

I made a promise
to the empty sky.
These three young ones
would not die.

Sosi

I rise before the sun,
before Mama can say no,
and go to the river
to see my vines.
I fill a basket with leaves
for *dolma*.
They must be picked
while still bright green
and supple,
each leaf the size of my palm
plucked from below
the new growth.

The apricots are hard and green
but soaking in the sun.
Soon they will be ripe.
Soon I'll be an auntie.

Mama's pacing on the roof when I return.
She takes the leaves from me and then,
as though we've never made *dolma* before,
as though I have not picked the leaves myself,
she tells me,

"They must be bright green
or else they'll be too tough."

She sets the black pot on the rooftop fire,
salted water inside it for blanching.
We excise the stems with sharp knives.
We set the leaves in the pot to wilt,
then pull them out to cool.

Mama mixes the filling.
Rice, olive oil, allspice,
cinnamon, and mint from the edge
of our stream.
    "Roll them tight, Sosi *jan,*
    tight as you can, Sosi *jan.*
    Fold the leaf edge in
    as you roll, Sosi *jan,*
    so the rice
    stays trapped
    inside."

Shahen

I wake before dawn
to church bells,
an urgent shake.
Mama, Papa, a goat,
and the butchering knife.

Papa says, "Bring your sisters to the highest field.
Tell them you are checking on the sheep.
Don't come back
unless we come for you.
Wait till it quiets,
then go south
to Aleppo.

"Stay high in the mountains,
heading southwest
till you see the desert
from the ridge.
Be careful when you cross the Euphrates.
Trust no one
till Aleppo.
Find the Forty Martyrs Church.
The *Soorp Hayr* there

helped your *keri*
get to New York."

He holds me for one second.
He wakes the girls.
Mama wraps a vest around me,
pulls me close in one motion, saying,
    "Wear this.
    It will keep you full
    and safe."
My head fits
into the curve
between Mama's head and body.
We pull in one breath together.
She pushes me away, looks me right in the eyes.
    "You are very young to be a man.
    Take good care of your sisters.
    Now go."
Mama wraps Sosi and Mariam
each in a new vest,
her hug squeezing
all breath from them.
Papa pulls her back,
puts Mariam in my arms,
adds a double knot
to the laces of the *charukh*
enveloping her feet.
    "Go now. They are coming."

"Who?" Mariam says.
Mama takes the pot from the table.
Papa pushes us through the door.
Mama follows.
Papa grips the goat and the knife.
Summer is here, but words
from springtime last year
come out from deep inside me.

    "Let's see who can get to the sheep first.
    Misak and Kevorg
    said we have new lambs."
Sosi looks back at Mama and Papa,
then at me.
    "We'll be back!" she says.
She grabs the black pot from Mama
and starts to run.

I run.
Sosi runs.
Mariam whimpers
as I squeeze her too tight,
her ear pressed to my chest,
her legs around my waist.
Behind us we hear the squeal
of the butchering of a goat,
followed by the death quiet.
I hear Mama
running toward the river screaming.

    "My girls, my beloved girls,

how could you kill them?
   You should have killed me instead."
We hear more screams
and sounds of guns from far away.
We hear soldiers near Mama.
We hear Mama's sounds
like an animal.
We hear Papa, near Mama.
   "No! You beasts! No!"
We hear soldiers and screams,
such screams.
We hear the sounds of our own breathing,
the sounds of our steps.
We run harder,
the noise of our hearts pounding,
blocking the sounds of home.
Footsteps, heart, and breath
fill our ears like rush of mill water at first thaw,
pushing up the mountain path,
our chests burning from the push,
in and out
legs up and down
our legs and hearts pounding
pounding
not stopping
till the top of the highest field.

Our ears fill with emptiness.
We drop to the ground.

I pull my sisters close together
behind the giant stone.
I find branches,
lean them against rock
to hide my sisters.
I crawl in
under branches
beside them.
They're both wet
from sweat
and urine
that poured from them
while they ran
and ran.

We are safe.

Ardziv

In the sky I circled,
head turning on neck,
eyes on young ones
running
soldiers
village
mountain
Mama
Papa
Anahid, big with child,
Palewan,
her mate's mother,
pushing her
toward a chest
in front of the house,
all of it
in my sight
as I circled,
talons ready to swoop
and attack
for the young one's sake.

Palewan said to Anahid,
   "Snakes in this village

will tell them who you are.
But if soldiers come
they will not find you.
I promise."
She kissed the top of her head.
She kissed her belly, filled with child.
She covered her with blankets.
She closed the lid.
Children
running,
shots,
screams,
Mama,
Papa.
The peal of bells stopped.
The smoke and smell of burning meat
filled the air.

On the hilltop,
behind the big rock,
Shahen covered his sisters
with branches.
He stepped out
to hilltop's edge
to see the valley
spread below him,
standing still as stone.
I circled.
Circled.

Shahen

I had to see.
From here
Papa always showed us the whole valley,
both sides:
the bridge
with its eight arches,
the green Euphrates
winding through the middle.
Smoke rises from our house.
Also from the Kacherians'
the Manuelians'
the Bagramians'
the Atamians'
the Garjians'
the Papazians'
the Evazians'
the Takoushjians'
the church
everything
Armenian
in smoke.

A new smoke plume curls toward the sky,
down the river.

The Garabedians'.
The soldiers are moving to the east.

I climb onto Papa's stone,
the one he lay on after a meal
every time we came here.
I feel him in the stone.
I make every part of my back body touch the
    stone.
Inside my head I hear Papa telling me
again,
Palu will be safe.
I curl and crush my bones
into the stone.
Palu was not safe.

Another plume of smoke
farther up stream:
the Ishkanians'
this time.

On the path I see them
bathed in bright white light.
Papa, Mama,
carefree,
carrying two baskets,
the mats,
Papa's *oud*.

They sit right in front of the stone
where we ate together,
always

singing,
laughing.
Papa plucks his *oud*
with an eagle's quill.
Mama spreads a feast on the ground in front of me.
Lahmajoon,
dolma,
madzoon.
Mama peels a peach,
then says,
"Shahen will be a good *keri*
to his sisters' children."

Our eyes meet.
She becomes a new smoke plume
to the east,
my bones cold
like a naked baby on that stone.

"South," Papa says
before he disappears.
"At night," I tell the empty space.
I know how to help us.
Night will be safe.

Ardziv

As soldiers swarmed the village,
Mustafa pushed Fatima
behind the garden wall
into a pen with the goats
waiting to be butchered.
He tied her hands and feet,
talking to his god as he worked.
    "Allah, forgive me for tying my wife's hands and feet.
    Allah, forgive me for putting a cloth in her mouth.
    Allah, forgive me for barricading the door,
    with Fatima behind it.
    Allah, forgive me."

He knew their deaths would stick to Fatima's soul
like a burr to silk trousers,
tearing the fabric with every step.
He knew Fatima would have said too much.
She would have told the soldiers
of the place the young ones ran to.
She would have told about Anahid,
and the chest would be opened.

Columns of smoke rose through the valley and met me
  in the sky,

Armenian homes burned,
some with families trapped inside.
The fields below the bridge
filled with soldiers
and Armenians,
their bodies
and heads
severed.
Again Mustafa said it:
    "Allah, forgive me,
    forgive me.
    Forgive us all."

Sosi

I wake to a stink:
branches over us
Mariam
slippery
smelly
Shahen
not here.

A searing ache
in the back of my throat
spreads
to every edge of my body.
I remember the morning.
Through branches
I see our land,
no one else here.

Mariam moves,
tries to cry.
I cover her mouth
tight and hard.
She listens to my hand.
We wait for Shahen.

Ardziv

The drum-capped soldiers
came to Kaban's.
He faced them
in his prayer shawl,
his brother, there from
Abder village, beside him.
Palewan sat on blankets
blocking the chest.
She smashed cumin seeds
with her pestle,
trapping them between
two hard surfaces.
The heads of the drum caps
stayed whole.

They questioned Kaban.
He sweated.
His hands shook.
But he looked them
in the eye,
never glancing
at his wife,
or at the chest

that sat behind her.
And they left.

Kaban ran to the chest,
opened the lid.
Anahid lay ashen and limp,
belly swollen with child.
They pulled her out.
They washed her,
dressed her in fresh clothes.
They removed her cross
from its necklace chain.
Palewan said,
"Go to Abder village now.
Kaban's brother will hide you there."
A month's supply
of pungent cumin
could not cover
the stench of people
burning
in their homes.

Mariam

Sosi hurts me.
My mouth.
It was the soldiers.

Mama.
Mama.
Mama.

Ardziv

Fatima crouched
in the corner,
hair wild,
wrists rubbed raw.
Mustafa set a pot of water beside her
and loosened the kerchief at her teeth.
    "Is it over?" she asked
through the cloth as it slacked.

She lifted knotted ropes
round her hands
toward his face,
like a child presenting
a tangled boot lace.
But when their eyes met
she knew
it was not.

Not then.
Not yet.
Not ever.

She dropped her hands.
She opened her mouth to speak.

But he filled it
with a ladleful of water.
She gulped it down,
and the next one
and the next.
She gulped
each ladleful of water
as he poured it
into her,
one after another
without a beat in between,
until the pot was empty
and he knotted the kerchief again.

Shahen ◆ *Sosi*

Sosi's fingers
dig into my arm,
her other hand tight
on Mariam's mouth.

Mariam better be
quiet if she ever
wants to see
Mama again.

I pet Mariam's head,
whispering,
"Os, os, os,"
like Mama did.

I let go
of her mouth
when she quiets.

Sosi's knuckles
are white
from grabbing
me so hard.

Shahen opens
my fingers
and I shake.

I leave one hand
on Sosi's,

the other
on Mariam's
soft curls.

Shahen says
night
will protect us.

I tell them
we'll stay here,
hidden,
till night,
then follow
the water
along the skeleton
of the earth
to the south.

I tell them
Mama and Papa
will find us there.

I feel Mama
beside me
breathing
in my ear.

I know
it is a lie.

"Look
in your pockets.
See the *dolma*

"Nuts

bastegh

coins

Mama."

in the pot?
Feel the seams."

"Nuts

halva

basturma

Mama."

Ardziv

Mustafa met Kaban
by the river
at sundown.
They found their bodies.
They washed them of blood.
It was worse for the wife.
Good they brought a cloth
to cover her.

Him, Papa,
the one I promised,
they slashed his throat,
the gash so deep
his skull hung on
by ragged bands of muscle only.
They each took one,
one body,
Mustafa him,
Kaban her.

She was wrapped in a cloth,
her clothes all gone,
her breasts severed,
her womb removed.

They carried them to Kaban's garden
to wash them,
to make them pure
for the grave,
Mustafa him,
Palewan her.
Kaban dug the grave.

As Palewan washed her she said,
    "Thank you, Allah,
    for sparing our grandchild.
    Thank you, Allah,
    for sparing Anahid.
    Thank you, Allah,
    for taking her from here
    so she never had to see
    what soldiers did to her mother."

Palewan washed her,
cleaned her,
made her pure for the shroud.
Under the smell of blood
rose the unmistakable smell
of man between her legs.
She washed this from her, too.

Rising moonlight
slanted through trees.
Shovel scraped

earth and rock.
They wrapped them
in simple shrouds.
They laid them together,
placing stones
in the shape of a cross
on top of them.

They covered the stones
with earth.
They transplanted mint
into earth
so no one would see
what lay below.

They buried Anahid's cross
separately,
inside a small ceramic bowl
from Abder,
with a fitted lid,
a very shallow grave
that they could find again.

Together they prayed for a time
when it would be safe
for the coming child to know
his mother was Armenian.

III

JOURNEY
Summer 1915

DAY 1
PALU

Sosi

To step hurts.
My legs shake.
Our clothes stink.
I can't go.

I can't leave this place
where Vahan will find me
with Mama and Papa.
But Shahen says,
    "No.
    Take the pot and go.
    We cannot go back.
    They told us to go.

    "In Aleppo,
    they'll find us,
    Mama
    Papa
    Anahid
    Misak

and Kevorg, too.
We need to be strong.
We need to go fast
in the dark,
time only for our needs."

We turn back to back.
I can tell from the sound
as his stream hits the earth
that he stands in his skirt while we squat.
Our streams fade
to quiet.
My ears strain
to hear.
Mama.
Papa.
Please come.
Come soon.
Take me back.

I rub the wool deep in my pocket
back and forth
between my thumb and first finger
till it burns.
Rays of the moon
light the stones on ground,
and I know,
and I know that

I
will
not
go
until
I pull
enough rough rock
to make the shape
of a cross
pointing south
for Mama
and Papa
to see
when they get here.
Together,
we'll find our way back.

Ardziv

I left the town
for good that night.
Without the sun
my sight is weak.
And raptors need both
speed and height.
Yet I kept my promise.
With weak moonbeams,
flying close to ground,
I tracked them as they moved.

DAY 2
SARYEKSAN MOUNTAIN

Shahen

The first night we stop many times
for Sosi to catch her breath,
for Sosi to unknot her cramping legs,
for Sosi to ask me more questions,
for me to tell her more lies.

Like a donkey,
I bear a balanced load,
the pot, lid sealed tight,
on one side,
and Mariam,
legs curled
round my waist,
on the other,
to go far before dawn
to Saryeksan Mountain,
up into the cold
away from our home.
Our sheep never grazed here.

We smell the spring before we see it.
We scoop fresh water
again and again
into our open mouths,
till new dawn brings back fear.

Sun and fear.
A maze of shepherds' paths
lead to this spring.
I take us uphill
away from the paths
behind some rocks
to try to steal some sleep
until the night.

I track the sun's course
across the blue sky.
The moon stays with us
through the morning.
Sosi and Mariam
sleeping, safe,
curled into a single ball
beside me.

I hear voices.
Sheep first,
then humans.
Let the bleats and bells hide us.

Bleats, bells, and bodies
will protect us
more than Papa ever could.
Shepherds better than soldiers.
Bleats and bells and shaggy wool
surround us
and hide us
more than this dress
ever could.

Mariam ◆ Sosi

"Sheep."

"Ma—"

"Get down!
Shepherds.
Shhhh!"

I cover her mouth,
her dry, sour mouth.
She shuts up.
Her eyes stare.
Bleats surround us.
Voices too.

Shahen covers us,
both of us,
with his body,
his small shaking body.
We sweat.

The ground is thick
with hooves.
The air is thick
with shepherds' words.
　"Stupid Armenian
　sheep, they

won't listen!
Look how
they stay alone,
acting like
they are better
than our sheep."

Ardziv

Sheep swarmed around them,
a wall of wool
twenty bodies thick.
With the sheep, two shepherds,
two young drum caps, Turks,
tending two flocks
now made one
by Ottoman guns.
One said,
    "Look at how these ones are greedy,
    taking all the best grass
    and crowding out our sheep."
He picked up a stone
and raised his arm to throw it
toward the young ones.
I swooped down,
grazed his head
with my left talon.
They shrank back
and looked up,
their eyes wide with fear,
their feet glued to the ground.
I made tight circles
in the sky just above them

three times.
I pulled up higher
and hovered
as they caught their
wits and breath,
building momentum,
making ready to attack
with a rapid descent.
I
shot
down.
They ran,
leaving their sheep
to me
to push the flock
away from this place,
down the slope
to their new masters,
to make the young ones safe.

Shahen

The ground shakes
with stepping hooves.
The sheep move off
as if chased.
A high, weak whistle
like a ghost in the wind
blends with bleats and bells.
Our cover disappearing
like water leaving
a pail with a hole.

I crouch before
Sosi and Mariam,
shielding them,
facing the spring,
the direction of the voices,
with one large stone
in each hand,
ready to strike them
when they find us.

If we live
I promise
I will run us harder at night,

but stop sooner
to find the safest place
to steal some hidden sleep
leaving no signs.

Woolly coats and bodies
thin around us
as the sheep march off
as if called
or pushed.
A high, weak whistle
comes from the sky.
Every fiber
under my skin
jumps.
Papa did this to us.
He put us in this danger.
He put me in a skirt.
And then he was killed
with an arrow made
from his own feathers.
Fool.

As the last sheep leaves
my vision clears.
Tails and rumps recede
down the mountain path.
The rest of the ground
is empty.

No shepherds.
No soldiers.
Just stone, brush,
and us.

Above,
against a pure blue sky,
a lone raptor,
an eagle,
circles.
He's here for the hunt,
no doubt.

Sosi

Hooves fade.
Whistling stays.
Heart like fast drum
in throat and ears.
Eyes shut.
Hands tight
on Mariam's
mouth
and eyes.

Shahen whispers,
    "They're gone."
I open my eyes.
It's true.
We're alone.

I whisper to Mariam.
She makes no sound,
her eyes like dark caves.
I take her to drink from the spring.
Shahen says we must go to Aleppo.
Yesterday he said that
Mama and Papa

would find us there.
Today he will not answer.

No. I won't go.
Not until I'm filled
with gulps and gulps
of water from the spring
and the tiniest bites
of *dolma* from the pot.
I let each lonesome grain of rice
linger
in my mouth.
Even cold,
I taste Mama
in every bite.

Ardziv

Shahen kept his promise.
From sunset
till the coming dawn,
he ran them hard,
as if to beat a storm.
As soon as the moonrise let me see them,
I flew up to the sky to find their forms
moving across the open mountain
above the tree line.
Each day the moon shifted to later.
Somehow they could see and move by the stars.
He kept them high on the mountains.
It was cold there,
with little food.
Each dawn they curled
like cubs in a burrow,
wedged between rock
or under some brush
where only an eagle's eye
could find them.

DAY 7
HAZAR MOUNTAIN

Sosi

The wool is thick and mottled
like a clot of blood
from the heat
and the wet
and the press.

With thumbs and fingers
I pull the fibers loose
till they break,
like we did
when carding wool
before spinning.

I pull tiny tufts from the clot
with my fingertips.
I let them rest and breathe,
a small red cloud
on my lap.

The cloud rests
on my chest as I sleep,

light as feather down.
The sleeping bird
did not die, Mama.

I return it
to my pocket
at dusk.

DAY 8
HAZAR MOUNTAIN

Shahen

The night sky and Father Manoog's maps
merge in my mind.
Each night I find the big bear
in the northern sky and run us,
the bear at our backs
over my left shoulder.
High Kurdish ridges
away from the rivers,
villagers, and food
bring us
from one cold mountaintop
to another.
Connecting woods surround us,
close us in,
protect us
from soldiers.
Invisible.

High areas open,
we stand out,

visible
by the late rising
crescent of moon,
shivering
against the whiteness
of rocks
above the tree line.

Faster, Sosi.
We must get to the Arab desert.
Desert
connecting to
seas
connecting to
America.

Safer cities near salt water
where we should have gone,
all of us,
months ago.

Ardziv

I've seen the Euphrates,
its full length,
all its branches,
many times
from the high springs
in the mountains near Van
running steep and fast
to the river's slow, flat flow
at its Persian Gulf mouth.
I knew its twists and turns,
how it carved a path
through the rock
to bring food and life
to all of us.
But I'd flown it
only by day.

To find Aleppo,
the Euphrates
had to be crossed.
I started spending
daylight's final hours
high in the sky,
committing the shape

of the river
and earth
to my mind,
to prepare
for the dark nights
as the moon slipped
from sliver
to nothing,
to find them again
when the light
returned
to the sky.

I knew what lay ahead
and behind,
the river flowing red,
the land teeming with vultures,
bands of *chetes* on horseback,
long lines of Armenian
women, children, and the old
driven by Ottoman soldiers.

Shahen chose the safety
of the darkest night
to cross the river.
I couldn't stop them.
I couldn't see.
They had to cross.
Only night
could protect them.

DAY 13
BETWEEN KEFERDIZ
AND CHUNKUSH

Mariam

Down to the river,
to summer.
This summer smells bad.
Rocks scrape my legs.
I hope Mama's there.

Shahen

We cross the Euphrates
on a moonless night.
Above the cold water
rushing between our legs
a thick smell hovers,
pulls my gut.
Our skirts float up
as we cross.
Mariam sits
on my shoulders.
Her feet dip into the bitter water
as it rises to my chest.
Muddy mounds
on the opposite shore
snap into forms.
Heaps of bodies
strewn on water's edge.
I pull Mariam
down into the water,
pressing her face to my chest.
Her legs drag through the water.
I grab Sosi's hand.
   "Close your eyes.
   Just hold on.

Keep them closed.
Like a game.
Just hold on."
Tied to her back,
the empty pot
starts to fill.
I turn it
so it empties.
   "I've got you.
   Hold on.
   Keep them closed.
   Just hold on."
I steer us
to the shore.
Water pours
from the pot.
Up the bank
past the bodies,
heaps of them,
bloated,
cut open.
   "Just hold on.
   Keep them closed.
   Hold on tight."
Throats slit,
whole families
dead together,
mothers,
old men,

198

daughters,
young boys.
    "Keep them closed.
    Just hold on.
    Ten more steps."
I let go only
when all they can see
when they open their eyes
are shadows
of muddy mounds.

I close my eyes and can see far away
to the heaps of young men,
their hands tied together
for their safety
till the trouble ends.
Shot
in a line,
falling
in a heap,
like the juice
from my stomach
that heaves
to the ground.

DAY 14

Sosi

It is day.
Time to sleep,
but I cannot.

If I close my eyes
I see them
by the river.

The smell
will never
leave.

I didn't mean to kill
the red bird.
I only cut the wool.

Mariam

Sosi sits
on the pot.
She won't speak.

Shahen beats
a stone
with a stick.

It breaks.
He gets another
and another,

still beating.
His lips
spit words

into the air.
   "Stupid.
   Papa.
   Fool."

DAY 15

Shahen

With each step
I grind small stones
into the earth.
Each stone
like Papa's head.
Papa's head.
Papa's head.
I step on it.
I kick it.
Fool.
Fool.
Stupid fool.

So little food.
The pot and pockets empty.
Now it's only seams
and coins we cannot spend.
How can we get there
with so little food?
With mountains

cold and barren?
Fool.

Mariam's lips
are drawn down,
her steps so short
and slow
I pull her up.
Her legs wrap
around my waist,
her arms around my neck.
Almost feather-light now,
she is asleep
in an instant.

Clouds block the stars.
I feel the river at my back
to know the way
back to the safety
of the mountains.

DAY 17

Mariam

Sosi gives me
three nuts,
three dried apricots,
and one small handful
of wheat
from the hem.
I want more.
She says no.
No more.
No more.

DAY 19
GERGER MOUNTAIN

Sosi

Opening the seams each day
for the food sewn inside by Mama
brings us close to her.
The imagined wrists,
the hem,
the two sides that come together in front,
surrounding me like Mama's arms.
The seams of the collar like her necklace,
filled with apricot flesh dried
and bitter nuts taken
from inside hard wrinkled pits
together on our roof
last summer.

I let the cracked wheat
from the hem
soften in my mouth
for hours

while we walk
and walk.

I never want to eat that last bite
from Mama.

DAY 21
GÜNGÖRMUŞ MOUNTAIN

Shahen

I pour the last bits of wheat
from the seam of my coat
into Sosi's open palm.
But something long and thin
still sticks in there,
light but firm.

Sosi divides the wheat
as I work it out
bit by bit.
Mariam's hungry eyes
stick to my coat
till it emerges:
a quill
from an eagle.
The *mizrap*.

What good is this?

Ardziv

He tossed my quill
into a bush,
his anger giving him the heat
and strength
he could not get
from food.
Hunters know this.
Our bellies are empty
when we chase.
Our wings
beat the air.
Our talons grab
and choke.
Fury does not leave us
till we eat.

Sosi

I say it's for my body's needs
and walk back to the place
where he threw it.
I pretend
and I squat.

The young moon rose
to help me find it,
catching the white
of the shaft
in its light.

The tapered, curved white line
divides the feather into two parts,
connected but unequal,
the spray of white down at its base
so soft in my palm.

Rich earth-brown feather fibers
like straight strong lines of fringe
from each side of the shaft,
widening, then tapering
to the tip,

where the feather has a pattern,
spots, almost stripes, of lighter color,
like petals or tiny leaves
dyed into its yarn.
I found this quill with Mama.

Papa held it in his hand
while we danced.
He will hold it again
for me to dance
with Vahan.

DAY 22
NEMRUT MOUNTAIN

Shahen

I drive us extra hard that night,
mashing Papa's head
into the earth
with each step.
Master of another barren
windswept summit
before dawn.

As earth and rock
give way
to broken stones
under us,
I see them to the east.

Massive headless stone bodies
sitting ramrod straight
in a row with a
pointed peak behind them.
Six of them,
feet evenly spaced.

And on the ground around them
huge heads sprout from the earth.
Heads without noses,
that one like Papa,
an eagle,
and a lion.

This can't be real.
It must be the hunger
playing tricks.
No Papa.
No quills.
No eagles.
But my sisters see them too.

Mariam

The eagle calls me.
Just his stone head.
He has no body,
just a giant head
rising from the ground.

I let go of Shahen
and go to him.
I kiss the tip
of his beak.

Sosi

A pagan temple.
It must be.
Gods forgotten
high on a mountaintop,
just as our God
has forgotten us.

Heads cut off
like those at the river.

I pull Mariam from the eagle.
We need to hide
before dawn comes.

Ardziv

The little one,
Mariam,
lay very still,
large, dark eyes wide open,
head flung back toward the sky.
She opened her mouth,
　　open shut,
　　open shut.
Then she swallowed the air
three times more,
　　open shut,
and she swallowed.

Just like a hatchling
she spoke to me.
I rose to the sky
for the hunt.

DAY 23
KOCAHISAR MOUNTAIN

Mariam

Look
Food
Rabbit
We have food.
Good
Food

Shahen

I strike one stone
with the edge of another
as I study the stars.
I brought us too far south.
We'll lose the safety
of the ridge this way.
We must go a bit north
as we go west.

My sisters do not
know the stars.
They won't know
I've added steps.

A sharp-edged flake
splits off. I slice into the
still-warm flesh,
lifting chunks of muscle
from the bone.
My sisters' mouths
are red with rabbit blood,
their white teeth gleaming.

DAY 24
ONUR MOUNTAIN

Shahen ◆ *Sosi*

We cannot eat snake.

Why not?
It's food.
We're hungry
and it's here
like a gift.

But snake?

It's not snake.
It's a gift.
Don't question it.
Just eat.

And why is it here?
Who would give
us a snake?

An eagle.

Don't be a fool.

I'm not a fool.
If we had fire
I'd make soup
in the pot.

But we don't.
Just eat.
It's good.
Like the back
of a lamb.

Lamb?

Yes.
Lamb.

Ardziv

As they starved
I hunted harder,
heading down
from the mountains
to valleys
warming
well into summer.
For five straight days
I placed small animals
on the ground
where they slept
just as the sun set.

The children woke
and ate them raw
before starting
the night's run.

But when a brown she-bear
with large curved claws
and pointed teeth,
ravenous from raising cubs,
caught the scent of blood

and began to trail them,
I had to stop.

Instead of leaving meat for them,
I left a trail
of small animals
for the bear and her cubs,
taking them far from the children.

DAY 30
KOÇALI MOUNTAIN

Sosi

When Mariam walks
on her own—
she does it less and less—
Shahen's hands rise
to his chin and lip
to search for hairs
that will never come,
not without food.

Shahen does not
need to know
my monthly blood
has stopped.

I am glad.
How would
I stay clean
here
if it
didn't
stop?

Shahen ◆ Mariam

Come here,
little bird.
Time to play
the bird game?

No.

Writing bird?

No.

Then I
will write
on you,
little bird.
Remember bird?

No.

What, then?

Mama.

Write Mama.

Mama:
swan down, wave,
smile, smile,
half smile.

Curve.
Smiles gone.

Swan down, wave,
curve, curve,
half curve.

           Mama.

DAY 31
ULUBABA MOUNTAIN

Sosi

First I ate the skin
by my fingernails.
Then I chewed
on a nail all night
while we walked.
Now my nails won't grow.
I chew a twig
and touch the quill
back inside a seam,
my seam,
where it's safe
as we walk.

I pull it out
when we stop
before full dawn
and Shahen goes
to search for food.
I touch Mariam's neck and face

with the quill's feathery tip
so she sleeps.

I touch my own
neck and face once
to remember
the shimmering
feeling of Vahan
before I put the quill back,
hidden from Shahen,
who cannot know I have it.

If he threw it away again
I might never find it.

DAY 33
BUZ MOUNTAIN

Shahen ◆ *Sosi*

The pot is heavy
and you are weak.
Let's leave it.

Leave something
that we have
from home?
Never.

You need
your strength,
Sosi *jan,*
for the journey.
The pot is heavy
and I need
my strength
to carry
Mariam.

Never, Shahen!
Never.
You wanted
to leave.
Not me.

This pot
is every meal
we ever ate.
This pot
is black
with the smoke
from our hearth.
This pot is Mama
and *madzoon*
and *dolma*.
It gives me strength.
From that,
you may
find yours.

DAY 35
BUZ MOUNTAIN

Shahen

Without olive oil, fire, and Mama's touch,
wild onions and garlic pulled from the earth
leave a sour tang in my throat.
Our stomachs cough up
yellow clumps
after we eat.

Mountain grass and flowers
are sweeter but cannot fill us.
The seams are empty like our stomachs.
Water from cold springs hits our insides.
Filling bellies with worms and bugs
empties our other parts.

I fill us with a story.

The first mother gave birth to the earth.
Like all good mothers,
she fed it with milk so it could grow.
In the sky you see her milk

flowing in a circle
around the earth.
When God saw how the earth had grown
so beautiful,
he filled it with his children.
He made Eve from Adam's rib.
Eve fed her children with milk
like the first mother
who gave birth to the earth.

Look at the sky.
You can always feel full
from drinking in *Dzir Gatin*,
the Milky Way.

DAY 36

Mariam

Ma:
Swan down, wave,
curve, curve, half curve.

Swan down, wave,
curve, curve, half curve.

Ma
Ma
Mama

Ma
Ma
Mama

Cold
Hungry
Mama

DAY 37
BORIK MOUNTAIN

Shahen

Mountain snows
melt with summer sunshine.
Streams rush.
Flowers bloom.
But this high up
it's still too early
for ripe fruits.

This wide stream glistens
from early moonbeams.
A voice inside it says
find water,
follow it to people.

We find a place
in the woods
for the girls to wait
one night,
one full day,
one half night.

I follow the stream.
I promise to return with food.
I tell them,
    "Leave
    if I'm not back
    by tomorrow night.
    Leave
    when the moon is high."
Sosi's brows knit
like thick black wool.
Like a burr from a field,
Mariam grabs my skirt.
She won't let go.
I pull apart her fingers.
    "I will come back.
    But if soldiers find me
    you must leave
    before they find you too."
The mounds by the river
rise here by this stream.
Sosi sees them too,
I know.
I tell her,
    "Go south.
    Use the stars.
    Stay high
    till you see the desert
    from the ridge."
Sosi's sharp bones

cut into me as we hug. She says,
    "You'll find us in Aleppo
    with Mama and Papa,
    Kevorg,
    Misak,
    and Anahid.
    Together we'll go home."
I nod.
She lets me go.

Sosi

The red cloud of wool
so soft and so fine
is ready to spin.
I pull a tiny pinch
between the tip of my thumb
and finger.
I rub it back and forth
between finger bones,
pulling as I rub.
Pull it out bit by bit,
rub it back and forth.
The red cloud becomes
a long red thread.
I can make it back
into a bird
again.
I must.

Mariam

Shahen.

Wave,
curve to the side.

Shahen.

Shahen

I follow the stream for hours
to some houses on its bank,
houses pink with dawn,
filled with other people and their food.
I retie my head scarf.
I watch from behind the trees
while women and girls
help men and boys
get ready to leave with the sheep.

I choose the one who smiled
as she gave her boy food.
I ask her,
not right away,
while the morning chatter continues,
Kurdish and Turkish mixed together,
but after,
when the women
go back to their houses.

I smooth my skirt.

I open her door,
Mama's coin in my open palm.
    "Please, mother.
    Do you have food for me and my sisters?
    Our village was burned.
    Our parents killed.
    Please, mother?"
She closes my hand around the coin and answers,
    "Come."

She pulls me inside
onto the warm soft carpet.
Colors rise through the soles of my feet.
Cinnamon surrounds me.
My mouth fills with wet.
She cuts a slab of cheese,
bread and olives,
hot tea
for me.
    "Eat slowly, so it
    stays down," she tells me.

Warmth flows
from my throat
to my toes
to my crown
to the tips of my fingers
with each swallow.
My belly's full so fast.

The bread and cheese
sit before me.

Inside a cloth she wraps
basturma
bastegh
cheese
halva
nuts
foods
rich
dense and dry.
They will take us
over mountains.
She asks no questions.
She wraps and ties the cloth
tight and secure like a swaddled child.
She folds the cheese inside the bread.
I put it in my pocket. Our eyes meet.
She sees through my dress and scarf to me.
She places one hand on the side of my head.
A kerchief cannot hide a mother's touch. She says,
    "Your clothes, they are good. Stay like this.
    Don't let them know. Hide till nightfall.
    Soldiers were here a few days ago."
My clothes.
My face burns.
If soldiers catch us,
what good could

these clothes do?
Soldiers would strip me
like all the girls at the river.
Girl after girl, naked.
I saw them.
Young boys died clothed.
I'd be stripped
and they'd know,
and then what?

Ardziv

I circled the village
all day while he hid,
rising high enough
to see Sosi and Mariam too.
Sosi pulled wool
into thread
as Mariam slept.
Lines of soldiers
marched in the distance.
Small groups combed
the woods
for strays
like Shahen,
Sosi, and
Mariam.

Sosi ◆ Mariam

Mariam wakes
in the dark.
She wants to run.
She expects it.

"*Yalla,*
come on.
We must
find Shahen."

I cover her mouth.
She quiets.
We go back
to the stream.
We drink.
We eat grass.
We wait.
We place stones
in a heap.
He's got to know
how to find us.
We listen
for Shahen's
footsteps.
Without running,
night is huge.

242

Wind
water
branches
breathing.

                                               "I want Shahen."

"Let's go back
to the wood.
Shahen went
to get food."
We wait till the moon
is high.
"Come closer.
I will draw
a story
on your back.
We are at home,
with Mama
making *lahmajoon*."

                                               "Lahmajoon."

"Shahen's happy.
Lahmajoon is
his favorite.

"Around the big
rolling stone
Mama breaks
off small pieces
of dough.
She gives one

to you, and a stick
Papa made smooth
for rolling.
You poke holes
in the dough.
Mama pushes
down hard.
She rolls the pin
front to back.
Rotate the dough
front to back,
rotate the dough."

                              "Mama."

"Circles of dough
go onto the tray.
I spread
meat
onions
peppers
tomatoes
and mint
on top."

                              "Mama.
                              Swan down."

"Yes. Mama.
She puts the tray
into the oven.
Meat and mint
perfume the air.

We make more
and more
and more.
She rolls the pin
front to back.
Rotate the dough
front to back,
rotate the dough.
Out of the oven
we stack them
into a tower.
We are ready
for everyone
when the mill work
is done."

                                    "Where's Shahen?"

I listen
for my brother's
footsteps.
The moon rises.
Night grows.

                                    "I want Shahen."

No footsteps.
My head aches.
My gut pulls
to nowhere.
I search the stars
for south.
I search the treetops

for the right branch,
ready to leave
without him
when the moon
touches it.

"Shahen, *goozem*."

The moon moves.
Shahen does not.
He'll never get here.
The moon
wins the race.
Soldiers may have
found him.
He won't be
in Aleppo.

I place two sticks
on the ground.
With a bit of red thread
I tie them into a cross.
I pull Mariam
to her feet.
I grab the pot.
"Time to run,
little one."

Shahen

It is dark.
Please, Sosi,
wait for me.
I can't go yet.
People wander outside
between and around the houses,
like we did at home
in summer
on the roof
at night,
singing,
dancing.
Cold air hits me,
makes me shiver.
I make it summer in my mind.
Summer on the roof,
apricot summer,
dancing the *tamzara*.
One—two—three,
stomp, stomp.
Full of life
for hours,
waiting,
Sosi and Mariam waiting.

Wait for me.
Please.
This village still stirs.
Those men
might be soldiers.
I cannot go.
I let my mind
join the line.
dancing the *tamzara*
with my brothers,
Mama, Anahid,
and Sosi.
Boy, girl, six in a line,
hands on each other's shoulders,
the sound of the *zurna*
piercing the air.
One—two—three,
stomp, stomp.
Kevorg,
Mama,
Misak,
Anahid,
then me
and Sosi.
Our hands slip to clasping.
The moon is too high.
Those men must be soldiers.
Why don't they sleep?
One—two—three,

stomp, stomp,
the bad things
leave us
as we stomp
on the roof.
One—two—three,
stomp, stomp.
One—two—three,
stomp, stomp.
Papa comes to the line.
He pulls me from it.
He says I'm a girl.
I push to join them,
Kevorg and Misak,
stomp, stomp,
content with the mill,
stomp, stomp.
I pull Papa's arm,
stomp, stomp,
from my shoulder.
One—two—three,
stomp, stomp.
Kevorg and Misak,
stomp, stomp.
One—two—three,
stomp, stomp.
Content with the mill,
stomp, stomp.
One—two—three,

stomp, stomp.
White faces
like clowns,
stomp, stomp.
The soldiers leave,
stomp, stomp.
I step out
like lightning.
The moon is too high.
My feet know the way.
I run alone.
Faster
without them,
white faces
like clowns,
to a steady pulsing beat,
to my sisters
in the woods
by the stream.

Sosi

I pull Mariam back to the stream.
Moonlight cuts through the trees,
lighting a clear white path in the
   water
rushing through the stone.

Oh, Mama, my Mama,
are you making *dolma*?
I've got the pot.
Papa, my Papa,
plucking the *oud*.
Misak and Kevorg
white from the mill.
Anahid, my sweet sister,
has your new baby come?
I hope it's a girl.
Girls don't leave.
I can hold your baby in my arms
and breathe in
the pure, sweet smell
from the top of her head
that I remember
from baby Mariam.

I put down the pot.
I pick up my sister.
I bury my face
in her stale, knotted hair.
Shahen can go to America
by himself.
I must go where
Vahan can find me.
I pick the pot up
and turn to the north.
We're going home.

Shahen

I fly down the stream bed,
searching each stone
for the place
where we turned
and they waited.

But I can't find the place
and the moon is too high.
I cannot call out.
Back in the village
those men,
they might hear me.

I cannot call out.
How can I find them?
Strong, bright moon,
help me, please.
Help me
find them.

A large bird
flies over me,
not an owl

or a bat.
It's a day bird,
an eagle,
out at night
like me.

Sosi

Without Shahen
night sounds grow.
Mariam heavy
like a sack of milled wheat,
the pot like a stone.
I follow the light in the stream
back to home.
More night sounds:
wind,
footsteps,
breathing.
Ours?
Shahen said,
    "If I do not come back,
    they'll be looking for you."
He said,
    "Go fast."
Stomp.
Stomp.
I go fast.
Back to home.
With the light
down the stream,
back to home,

where I'll find them
waiting for me.

The eagle passes over us,
then turns and comes toward us,
flying upstream
as we go down,
coming close to my head,
the strong flap of wings
beating like the *dumbek*
and a strange whistling sound,
its cadence starting high,
then gliding down and fading,
like someone begging.
Again he comes over us
and makes a tight turn,
his beating wings and whistle
filling my ears.
But I won't turn around.
We're going home.

Shahen

I've gone past the place
where we turned,
I am sure,
so I retrace my steps
on each stone,
going slow
till I see it.

I missed it before:
a pile of stones
in a heap
at the stream,
left just for me
by my Sosi.

I leave the water's edge
and turn into the woods
till I find the soft spot
where they waited.
And there on the ground
where my sisters once sat
is a cross of two sticks
tied with red thread
pointing north.

North!
Sosi, no.
They will find you
and kill you.
Not north.
Not the river.
Not the soldiers.
Not north.
There's a bear in the sky.
Run away.
Run away.
Not into his claws
and his teeth.
Cross in my fist,
I run back
to the stream
as if the earth
is made of fire.

Step, step, step, step,
breath, breath, breath, breath,
step, step, step, step.
Then from that steady pulse
I hear it in my mind,
baron Kaban's *duduk* winding
da dee da dee da dee, daaa, da da dee da
da dee da dee da dee, daaa, da da dee da,
the drum pulsing,
the *Alashkerdi kochari*

calling me into a line of men
shoulder to shoulder.
Step,
     hey,
step,
     hey,
step,
     hey,
step,
     hey,
our call back to the drum
     syncopated,
the drum pushing my steps,
the *duduk* winding
da dee da dee da dee, daaa, da da dee da.
Step,
     hey,
step,
     hey,
step,
     hey,
step,
     hey,
faster and faster,
all in a line
we shift
into double time.
I fly across the earth.

Wings whoosh.
Eagle flies low
over streambed,
moon striking
his feathers,
and talons fierce.

Sosi

I hear footsteps
coming after us.
    Stomp.
    Stomp.
    Coming.
Purple light washes through the sky.
Stars fade.
I'm not fast.
I must hide us.
    Stomp.
    Stomp.
Quiet, Mariam.
  Stomp.
  Stomp.
  Closer,
breathing.
  Stomp.
  Stomp.
My eyes
close tight,
my grip on Mariam
tight as my eyes.
We do not breathe.
  Stomp.

Stomp.
They're coming.
  I want to go home but I can't.
  It's over.
Stomp.
Stomp.
Coming closer.
My eyes are shut tight.
My arms firm,
squeezing Mariam
to my chest.
But she squirms
and she breaks
from my arms.
I cannot hold her back.
They will shoot her.
How will I tell Mama?
I hug the pot to my gut.
I pray they shoot me first.
Someday, Mama
will meet me in heaven.
I hope I can tell her
they shot me first.
Then she will tell me
what happened with the goat.
I open my eyes
to see,
to tell Mama
about my end.

I see Shahen,
Mariam
in his arms,
coming
to pick me up too.

Shahen

"Sosi, you fool!
What were you thinking?
Don't ever go north.
There are bears in the north,
hungry from sleeping
and raising their cubs.
They wait by the river.
The bears, they will eat you.
You're running right into their
    mouths.
Don't ever go north.
Papa said to go south.
I said to go.
Listen to me.
I'm the man here.
Listen to me.
No more north.
Promise me.
No more north.
No more.
No."
Sosi nods.
    "Good.

264

"You went fast.
But I caught you.
I caught this for you.
See what I have?
Bastegh
basturma
bread
cheese
nuts
halva.
Eat, sweet sister,
eat.

"*Os, os, os,*
little Marig,
you were good,
you saw me.
You saw me.
We have food now.
A kind mother gave us food,
dense food.
It will stick to you like I do.
It will keep you warm.
It will give us many days
to go south
to Aleppo.
Never go north.
Never.

"Eat, sweet sister,
eat.

"North there is nothing.
Never was.
Nothing."

DAY 41

Mariam

Sosi gives me
a piece of cheese,
some flat bread,
so many nuts,
a big piece of spicy *basturma*,
a piece of shiny *bastegh*
like Mama's,
and a piece of sweet, sweet *halva*.
I fly through the woods
to Aleppo.

DAY 42

Mariam

Sosi gives me
a piece of cheese
some bread
some nuts
basturma
bastegh.
No *halva* today.
The hard bread
turns soft and sweet
in my mouth.

DAY 43

Mariam

Sosi gives me
five small pieces of cheese,
each of them wrapped
with a ribbon of *basturma*,
and *halva* for dessert.
The ribbons taste pretty.
I want more.

Sosi

Each day
I give Shahen
some of my share.
He must stay strong
to carry Mariam
when she tires.
I carry the pot.
His eyes like
a prison guard's
follow me
always.
These gifts
he does not see.

DAY 44

Mariam

Sosi gives me
three pieces of cheese,
only three,
very small,
and three large nuts,
each of them wrapped
with a ribbon of *bastegh*.
Sleepy
me.

Shahen

I should have asked
the mother for more
or taken it.
She had more,
plenty more.
I could have carried more,
much more.
But it looked like so much
when she gave it to me.
Almost gone now.
No going back.
And would Sosi stay
if I went
for food
again?

DAY 45

Mariam

Sosi gives me
two small pieces of cheese,
two nuts,
and one thin piece of *basturma*.
No ribbons.
She tells me
halva
again
tomorrow.
I eat slow.
I walk slow.

DAY 46
ENGIZEK MOUNTAIN

Mariam

Sosi gives me
one nut,
one thin piece of *bastegh,*
and a bite of *halva.*
No cheese,
no bread,
no *basturma,*
no Mama,
no Papa,
no.

DAY 47

Mariam

Sosi gives me
one big nut,
one thin piece of *basturma*,
and one tiny pinch of *halva*.
Shahen carries me.
My wings won't flap.

DAY 51
AHIR MOUNTAIN

Shahen

We each eat
one last pinch of *halva*,
and the food
from the mother
is gone.

This bare mountain
offers nothing but stones,
steep stones to climb
and small stones like candies
that would break our teeth,
already soft in our swollen gums,
if we dared to take a bite.
The night eagle soars above us.
His strange whistle
blends with the wind.
It's colder as we climb
above the tree line.

More wind,
the smallest sliver of moon,
almost set.
Mariam
tied to my back
with the cloth
from the mother,
emptied of food,
gone
to feed our bellies.
Mariam heavy
even with no food.
She warms my back.
Sosi carries the pot,
heavy,
empty.

This must be the last one,
the last mountain,
this must be.
Father Manoog's maps
still shine the way to the top
in my mind.
I want the crumbs
from his beard
here with me now.
Soon the sky will open.
We will see

through the desert
to Aleppo.

If we were goats
scrub grass would fill us.
Our hooves could grab rocks.
But I'm not a goat
and I slip.
I fall.

"Sosi!"

Sosi

Shahen screams my name
just once.
Falling stones echo.
Steep rock surrounds us.
I call back.
I hear nothing but Mariam crying.
Mariam in a ball
tied to his back.
I rush down in the dark.
In the dark, down is harder.
Up is climbing to weak moonbeams.
Down is stepping to emptiness
ending in the rock below.
I count each step.
Forty.
Till I find them with my ears.
They are wedged deep in a dark crack.
Mariam whimpering.
Shahen silent.
I sit on stone's edge, stretch down my feet,
but my toes cannot touch them.
Mariam wails. Holding one end,
I drop the ball of thread down to her,
small red ball in her hand in my mind.

I sing Mama's song till she stills.
I tear out the lining from my coat,
the seams once filled by Mama.
I wait till dawn's light on distant branches
calls me from the summit
to find a long branch
to
reach
down
to
them
stuck
between
the
stones,
Shahen's
head
on
stone
pillow.

Sosi

Good girl
come off his back
good girl
use the stick
pull the cloth the mother gave us
make it loose
come off his back
let the cloth
be his blanket
good girl
take the lining
of my vest
from the stick
wet your lips
suck on it
drink it in
good girl
fold the lining
find a clean spot
for Shahen
wet his lips
wipe his forehead
good girl
gentle

Shahen's head
good girl
fold the lining
wipe the cut
stay on the edges
good girl
touch his temples
trace the cut
kiss the cut
that's right
good girl
lick the cut
for you
hungry girl
good girl.

Shahen

Soldiers with guns
poking me,
pointing.
   "You, girl,
   over there
   with the other girls."
Poking
guns pointing
pointing with guns
poking my dress
poking Misak
poking Kevorg
insisting.
   "We have a paper."
Pointing with guns
poking them
poking me.
"You come with us."
Poking them
poking me.
   "You are not a girl."
Poking Misak
poking Kevorg.
Three shots

and we are gone.
Papa shakes me.
He has the goat
by his throat.
Not the goat.
Not the goat.

Mariam

Wake up,
Shahen.
Come back.
Open your eyes.
Come back.
There are no goats.
It is safe.
No goats.
Wake up.
Please.
Wake up.

DAY 52

Sosi

Dawn.
The skin of my palm
gathers toward
the hard quill tip
when I push it in.
I let go.
My skin settles back,
leaving only
the print of a small
circle in my palm.
The quill's feathery end
like Mama's touch
leaves no trace
on my skin.
Back and forth
on my arm
I touch.

Air whispers
quite near me

as the eagle lands on stone
just as if I called him
with the quill,
his quill,
the one I found
with Mama,
the one that Papa held
on our roof
while Misak and Kevorg
danced
and I poured
my secret
into Anahid's ear.

He's so close
I see the second
thin veil of lid
covering
his yellow eyes.
Short golden feathers
on his head and shoulders
shimmer
in morning light.
Above his claws
fine tufts
of red-gold down
sprout
as though he wears
short pants.

He moves his head
to the right,
pointing down the hill
as if to coax me,
to show me.
He takes two steps.
Wings whoosh him into flight.
I put the heavy stone
on top of the end of the thread,
the other end with Mariam.
I take the black pot in hand,
call to Mariam and Shahen
that I'm going,
that I will follow the eagle
back down the mountain path.

Shahen

Mariam's ancient eyes
stare into mine.
Where is Sosi?
She calls me from above,
her face
surrounded
by blue sky.
A thin red thread
connects us.
Heaven?

Sosi

Back down the mountain
I find soft earth
and new spring leaves.
Flowers tell of fat bulbs
underground.

In the day I can find
all the things
nature hid.
It's good I came out
in the day.

I loosen the earth
with small sharp sticks.
A circle of holes
encloses
leaves and stem

where soil
meets air.
I grab.
I twist
and pull,

poking a stick
into the ground,
where it holds
the roots of the
thick, fleshy bulb

we need
tight to the earth.
I want it more.
The earth
it gives.

I collect the bulbs
in my dress.
I wash them
in the mountain spring.
I eat some,

a juicy nut taste
tingling
my tongue.
I put the rest
into the pot

on top of
curled fern tips,
a mound of
fresh green spirals
like a nest

for the bulbs,
round and resting eggs.
I carry them
up the mountain
for Shahen and Mariam.

I pass the pot to Mariam,
its handle knotted to the stick
with a strip
from the hem of my dress.

"*Ardziv jan,*
thank you,"
I say to the sky.
"Tomorrow
I'll get even more."

DAY 53

Shahen

My head
heavy
hurt
on stone pillow
memories throb
from bloody lump.
I missed a step.
I fell
down
down
landing
belly and hands
first
Mariam
on my back
not under
safe.

Memories throb
from hardened heart

of Papa
and Mama
the goat
and the butchering knife.

Blue sky opens
above rock walls
eagle
sky
sky
sky
sky
sky
eagle
sky
sky
sky
sky
sky.
He flies small, tight
circles above me.

DAY 54

Sosi

Strong now
Shahen stands
on the pot.
Tall now
like Papa,
he holds Mariam high.

Day now
I lie flat on the edge of the crack
and stretch my arms down.
Shahen pushes Mariam up
till we touch.
Our hands meet.
I pull her up and out,
straight up to stand
with this brave small girl.
I squeeze her so tight
her thin bones might break.
She buries her head in my chest,
grinding her temples

back and forth
into my breastbone.
Bone to bone.
   "My girl,
    my girl,
    my sweet little girl."

She stops rubbing,
looks into my face.
The dull in her eyes
starts to warm
like sunbeams
down on my back.
Her eyes ringed with dark,
her hair thin and flat,
she turns up the edge
of her cracked lips
to a smile.
But before it can spread
her eyes flash.
Burning hot shoots through my feet,
kicked out from under me.
We crash to the ground.
She is yanked from my arms
twisted behind me.
I'm pulled from the edge.
My face scrapes on stone.
No.
No.

I twist round to see.
My shoulder blazes.
It's one man,
just one man,
one twisted face,
spit round his mouth.
Sharp black hairs
sprout from his ears,
Mariam under his arm.
    "Shahen,
    Shahen!"
    Mariam screams
    "Shahandukht," I tell him.
    "Our sister.
    Just a girl,
    Injured.
    She will die.
    She's stuck in the crack.
    We can't get her out.
    Three sisters.
    Just leave her.
    Let her die.
    She'll die.
    Just take us.
    She will die."
The man ties us together,
goes back to the edge,
and he snorts
and he spits

in the crack.
He stoops,
grabs a stone,
throws it into the crack
with such force
that it hits with a whack.
From below,
from my Shahen,
not even a whimper
floats up.
The only sound
the beat of wings.

Shahen

Face down
in the dark
skirt spread
out wide
inside
every muscle
fiber tense
like a shield
outside
seeming
almost dead
and a girl
almost dead
to him
to the gob
of spit
that hits
my head scarf
acting
almost dead
to the stone
that burns
a hole
in my back.

I do not flinch
acting
almost dead
almost
dead.

Sosi

Man turns
   Shahen safe
   Shahen strong
Man walks
   Shahen safe
   Shahen strong
Man here
   Shahen safe
   Shahen strong
Man cuts
   Shahen safe
   Shahen strong
my dress
   Shahen safe
      Shahen strong
Man drools
   Shahen strong
   Pot up
Man strips
   Shahen up
   Shahen walks
Man pants
   silent walk
   Shahen strong

Pot hands
Pot up
Crash down
Man falls
Blood pours
on me
on Mariam
on me
on Mariam
heavy man
on us
 Shahen strong
 pulls man
 by legs
 over stone
 into crack.
 Man gone
Shahen here
Shahen here
Shahen here.

Shahen

The first word comes
  "Os,

  os, os, os,

Sosig

Mariam

Sosig

Mariam

He's gone.

He can't hurt you.

He's gone.

You were smart,

my Sosig.

You saved me

your sister

my Sosig

so smart

my sister

three sisters.

You saved us.

You

Mariam

Me."

Sosi ◆ Shahen

"No, Shahen. You.
You saved us, Shahen.
You and Papa."

"Papa?
He had nothing to do
   with it.
He put us here
with that man,
that bloody man.
We should have left Palu
before any of this."

"It's our home, Shahen.
Our home.
How could we leave it?"

"Now his blood
is on our hands."

"That man would kill us."

"On Papa's hands."

"Papa's hands.

"Papa,
Mama.

304

Where are they?
I need to know.
Where's Mama?
Where's Papa?
What happened with the goat?"

Shahen

I step back to the crack
and look down inside
to where the man lies
still as stone
except for the pulse of his breath.
　　"Don't you know?"
Her body trembles with knowing
as she shakes her head no.
She holds Mariam tight.
She knows what happened.
I don't need to say it.
She saw death today.
She knows.
She must know.
　　"Mama and Papa killed the goat,
　　ran toward the soldiers
　　covered with its blood
　　so soldiers thought we were dead."
I hear Mama's sounds like an animal
and hear her screaming,
　　"You should have killed me instead."
　　"And then the soldiers killed them,
　　so we had time to run."
Sosi's fingers press hard on Mariam's arms.

Soundless tears drip from chin to chest.
Between us
I see whole families
wailing
at river's edge.
The pot's metal handle
cuts into my palm.

Sosi ◆ Shahen

"They won't be
in Aleppo?"

"They won't
be there. No."

"We'll never go back."

"There's nothing
to go to.
They burned
all our homes."

"I didn't want to know."

"I know."

"Misak and Kevorg?"

"They shot them,
I think."

"Anahid?"

"We can pray
that they
saved her."

"They did.
I can feel it.
We'll find her
someday.
She had her baby.
A girl, I think.

Her marriage
was good.
Papa was right."

"Papa right?
If we'd left
when I wanted
they wouldn't
be dead.
We have only this
heavy empty pot."

This pot,
solid, black, hard,
heavy in my hands.
This pot,
Mama's pot.
I pull it to my gut.
Hard metal
pangs shoot
up and down
my spine.
Mama's pot.
My tongue thick,
metallic,
wet.
We have it.
It's ours.
For the first time,
I see it

this precious pot,
this useful pot,
black and hard
like a cannonball.
We have this pot,
a solid heavy pot.
　　"Mama's pot."

"We have more,
Shahen *jan*.
I have you
and Mariam.
We have
Mama's coins.
We have the wool
from my
dowry carpet,
respun into
a thin red thread.
In America,
I will make
a new bird
in a carpet
for you.
Keri waits for us
with his sons
tall like plane trees
who speak English
like princes.
We are going

310

with you to America,
Shahen *jan,*
Mariam and me.
And look,
I saved
the quill.
It's going, too."

Shahen

From the seam at her collar
Sosi pulls out the *mizrap*,
the one Papa used to teach me.
She touches my arm with it.

Papa's melody
whispers inside me.
She places it in my palm.
My fingers close around it.

My heart hears the steady beat
of the *dumbek*. My lungs know
the *duduk*'s constant breath.
Papa's song surrounds me,

fills me, its steady pulse
always here, flowing through me,
shaping my insides
like water on stone.

The truth hidden
by my mountains
at last becomes clear.
We are here and alive,

we three sisters,
crossing oceans
because of Papa
and Mama.

"More of them may come.
Let's go now.
Together we'll run
to America."

DAY 61
SIMĀN MOUNTAIN

Sosi

From the final rise
a long flatness stretches.
The horizon fades and blurs.
Our climb done,
lights dot the desert.
Specks of light
must be
villages,
cities.
Aleppo?

At dawn, I look back to the north
across the sky-scraping mountains.
Miles behind them, in our fields by the river,
the sun makes my grapes sweet.

Morning light increases
the empty space ahead:
baked brown earth,
plants burnt or chewed,

so little green,
so far to cross.

With lily bulbs in our pockets, we gather stones.
Shahen makes the shape of a cross
pointing south to the church in Aleppo.
Mama and Papa can see from above,
like the eagle, he tells us.

We drink our last drops from the mountain spring,
soak and squeeze the ragged cloth to fill the pot.
We wet our clothes to suck on and keep cool.
Each step down, hot air rises to meet us.
When I spill precious drops he takes the pot.

He gives me Mariam.
He takes the pot.
We drink from the pot,
our clothes bone-dry.

DAY 63
BURJ HAYDAR

Shahen

With no place to hide from the sun, we move.
Piercing rays beat our brains to steamy hot.
Our mouths like sand, salty sweat streaks our cheeks.
Papa told me to follow the water.
Dry desert rivers make brown bands in sand.
Distant dust clouds shimmer with white flashes.

Do I see or imagine
ancient churches
rising from the earth?
Stone arches and walls crumbling,
columns without roofs.
Sosi falls and drops the pot.
I curl her fingers round the handle
and carry little Mariam

to the stone wall,
and know that it is real
from the shade

that it gives to my sister.
Empty ruined churches,
with no signs of who used them.
I go back for Sosi
and the pot. They sleep.
I follow the dry riverbed.

From brown and green specks
mixed with distant white,
Papa, my Papa, whispers to me,
    "*Hos egoor.* Come here."
Eagle flies to Papa's voice.
I step on dry river stones,
waves of heat rising
from folds in sand.
My leather *charukh* is worn paper thin;
each hot step burns.
I beg my feet to step some more.
I see a man, his son, and their camels.
A white cloth roof rises above their cart.
The boy in white coaxes the animals:
    "*Yalla, yalla.*"
Come on,
come on,
just like we said to our sheep.
Yalla.

The father peers out from the white cloth shade.
Like Papa's, his eyes are dark and deep.

I pull the Arab greeting from the crack
in my head that was filled before we fled.
  "*Sa'alaam al leik um*—may peace be with you."
  "And with you peace," he replies.
Buzzing flies cease their sound
as we stare past my rags
and his robes into pure dark eyes.
Dark and deep like Papa's.
He hands me a fresh wet cloth and a cup.
Their wetness brings Aleppo to my lips.
  "*Halep,*"
  he replies,
all other words mysterious.
I draw a cross.
He nods,
his eyes
edged in wrinkles
from years of smiling
under the Arab sun.
His eyes wrap me
like a blanket,
covering every raw edge.

  "*Yalla Halep,*" he tells me.
  "*Yalla.* Sosi, Mariam," I tell him.
My hands
measure the air
to show their height.
My palms move

together under my head
tilted, eyes closed.
Sosi and Mariam,
my sisters,
asleep in the sand,
waiting.
He sees them.
   "Yalla, Sosi, Mariam.
   Yalla."
Camels unfold
their legs and rise.

Camel hooves
and wheels of the cart
cover my steps.
Flames of sun
beat the sand
to burning hot.
Stone walls shimmer
in the distance.
The eagle
circles above.

They breathe
but cannot speak
when we find them.
We squeeze
drops of water
through cracked lips.

We lift them
to the shade of the
white cloth roof,
fresh wet cloths
on their heads,
drips on their mouths.

For final steps,
we three are
piled and pulled
to safety.
Sosi,
Mariam,
me,
safety.

ALEPPO
AUGUST 1915

Sosi

I wake in a bed,
surrounded by white cloths
stirring in hot wind,
Mariam tucked beside me.
Shahen?
Where is Shahen?
I call him.
I try to get up.

A woman in white
with a heavy wood cross
around her neck
runs to me.
She tells me he's well
with the boys again,
asking for me every day.
She tells me Mariam
does the same,
that now she's only napping.
She gives me a drink

and goes for him.
I pet Mariam's soft clean curls.
I whisper *"Os, os, os,"* like Mama did.
Mariam sleeping
thin
pale
sleeping
safe.

"Sosig," says Shahen,
still small,
head bare,
in trousers.
He pulls me so close.

"Mariam *jan,*" Shahen says.
"Wake up, little bird."

Mariam

Sosi
Shahen
Bread
Tall stick, small snake
Smile, smile, half smile
Half smile, wings
Bread.

IV
1919

ALEPPO
SPRING 1919

Shahen

War is done.
We wait,
me with my
Arab *baba*.
He took us in,
all three of us,
when Ottoman orders
came to march
the older orphans
into the desert
and to make the
young ones Turks.

To stay safe,
we dress as Arabs.
Sosi wears a hijab,
her head and neck covered;
I wear a *thobe*
over my pants,
a *keffiyeh* on my head.

We each keep
a smooth round coin
from Mama and Papa
tucked into the lining
of our clothes,
one a piece.

We work in the shop
in the Souq al-Attareen
selling nuts and spices.
Me out front,
Sosi and Mariam
grinding
in the back.

Each day we saw
the battered marching
to the desert,
to Deir el-Zor,
what could have been
our fate
but wasn't.

Each night
we shelled
pistachios
for those
who starved,

small, dense food
to sustain them.

The Near East Relief man
reads the names on letters.
No mail could move
beyond the Ottoman borders
for all the years of war.

Each orphan prays
for living family.
Sosi, Mariam, and I
have each other.
But to find Keri too,
my old dream.

Papa would be proud.
I found a street in Aleppo
with a tea shop
where a man
plays his *oud* sometimes.

My fierce left hand
learns the notes.
I have no neck to hold
or strings to press.
But I tap the patterns
onto my leg
as I watch him.

At the shop,
when it is quiet,
I practice
on the counter.
Between songs,
I push my fingertips
onto the counter's sharp edge
to make my calluses strong.

When I hold the quill,
Papa's quill,
loose between
my fingertips,
the *duduk, oud,*
and *dumbek*
blend into
a rooftop song.

I dream of Keri.
We wait for him.
But finding us
could be too much luck
for one family.
Others here have
no one
anywhere.

Three seasons of apricots
have already passed.

Baba gives us dates.

We are clean and well.
He takes us
to the mosque to pray
so no one questions
who we are,
each bow
followed by
forehead
chest
left
right
and three taps
on my heart
in my mind.

My sisters grew again.
I did too.
I'm taller than Sosi.
And bristles,
I have some.
Mama would smile.
We are the lucky three.

With each name read
by the Near East man
I shrink
until I hear it.

Shahen Donabedian.
My Arab *baba* hugs me.

The relief man says it again
before I can breathe
and stand.
Shahen Donabedian.

A letter from our uncle
with tickets
to America
for Mariam
for Sosi
for me.
A letter from our uncle,
our *keri*,
our precious treat.

Through the window
in Aleppo
it's as if I can see
from pale pink rocks
above the green Euphrates
beyond that, to the desert.
And beyond that, beyond that,
all the way to the sea.

Ardziv

Shahen, Sosi, Mariam,
on ship's deck,
rising sun and stretch of sea
behind them.
The statue's lighted arm
stretches up into the sky,
her feet still in shadows,
the points of crown like talons
against the blueing black.

Behind her
buildings scrape the sky
like mountaintops,
their lights like stars on earth.
Shahen tells them,
"You can climb up her arm
and inside the torch
to see houses
side by side
spread across the land
like vines in an orchard."

Three young ones,
one black pot,
a single quill,
and a tuft of red wool
are enough
to start a new life
in a new land.
I know it is true
because I saw it.

Author's Note

This story began, as many stories do, with a conversation. A sentence from that long-ago conversation has haunted me since I was a little girl. I asked my mother about her mother's childhood in western Armenia. She replied, "After her parents were killed, she hid during the day and ran at night with Uncle Benny and Aunt Alice from their home in Palu to the orphanage in Aleppo."

My grandmother Oghidar Troshagirian died long before I was born. My grandfather Yeghishe Mashoian, also a genocide survivor, died when I was six. Uncle Benny and Aunt Alice were colorful characters in my childhood, but I knew little about their lives. In my family, we didn't speak about the genocide. My mother married an American, so my brother, my sister, and I grew up speaking English. By the time I thought to ask the serious questions, that generation was gone.

I know little of how my grandmother and her siblings survived. I know that from Aleppo, with the help of a *keri*, a maternal uncle, they made it to New York. Somehow, a pot came with them—my American relatives argue over who has it. I know that they were millers from Palu. One older brother escaped to the east. An older sister was married to a Kurd.

Her grandson now owns a Turkish restaurant in The Hague, in the Netherlands, and a hotel in Antalya, Turkey.

Long before I ever imagined that I might write this story, I filled in the gaps of my family history by reading everything I could about the Armenian genocide: accounts by eyewitnesses, such as Henry Morgenthau, the United States ambassador to the Ottoman Empire from 1913 to 1916; oral histories; memoirs; academic tomes; and works of historical fiction. Still, I wanted more.

In the summer of 1984, my husband and I traveled to Palu. An unmarked Armenian church perched on the top of the hill above the town, its roof missing and its walls defaced. In town, vendors peddled *ayran*, the cool yogurt drink Armenians call *tahn*. We asked if there were any mills nearby and were sent across a modern bridge, built next to one of crumbling stone with eight arches. We followed the river's bank to a fast-flowing stream, then headed up the stream into the woods until we reached a mill with a series of attached buildings running up the slope.

On the rooftop of the largest building, the head-scarfed lady of the house served us sweet tea in clear glass cups. A half-dozen children with big brown eyes watched and listened. Mounds of apricots dried in the sun. She said that the mill had been in her family for sixty years; before that, it had belonged to Armenians. With anti-Armenian stories running in Turkish newspapers that summer, and all visible traces of Armenian inhabitants systematically denied or destroyed, I had kept my identity hidden as we traveled. But I told her the truth. We held each other's gaze as the water hit the mill wheel and the stones of the stream. The official Turkish policy of genocide denial evaporated for one brief moment on that rooftop.

The form of this story chose me rather than the other way around. Everyday language cannot express the scale and horror of genocide. Severed heads, rape, rivers red with blood, stinking heaps of dead bodies; the living emaciated, naked, sunburned, marching through the sand—we all turn away. I could only put it onto paper in fragments that slowly accumulated into a story. The eagle, Ardziv, and his magic came into the story to make it safe for me, for the reader, and for the young ones as they traveled. Three-quarters of the total Armenian population, about 1.5 million people, died in this genocide. Only luck, miracles, and perseverance saved the few who managed to survive. More than just a magical being, Ardziv embodies the strength of spirit that lives inside us.

If magical realism makes up this story's warp, then historical facts are woven into its weft, starting with the rooftop where I sipped tea. Various beetles have been used as carpet dye in the Middle East for centuries. The *oud* was traditionally played with an eagle's quill. The terrible facts of the genocide are also real. During the first half of June 1915, all the Armenian men of Palu, along with ten thousand men from nearby Erzerum, were slain by *chetes* on or near Palu's eight-arched bridge. Aleppo was a central staging ground for deportees from all over the empire who were then marched into the desert of Deir-el-Zor to die. Armenians from regions near to the then partially complete Baghdad Railway line were packed into cattle cars and brought to Aleppo.

The journey of Shahen, Sosi, and Mariam is entirely imagined, though with the benefit of many hiking trips in the cold above the tree line. They stayed along the ridge lines of real mountains and passed through archaeological sites such as mystical massive stone heads on Nemrut Mountain and the Byzantine ruins known collectively as the Dead Cities of Syria. When the Turkish state was founded in 1922, many place names were changed. Kharpert, the city where Shahen would have gone to college, is now Elâzığ. Constantinople is today's Istanbul. To map the young ones' journey, I linked today's names to those from the time of the genocide.

International relief work in the Ottoman Empire had begun during the Hamidian Massacres of 1895 to 1896, with Clara Barton, national hero, nurse, and founder of the American Red Cross, leading the American efforts. As the violence intensified in 1915, so did international aid. In Aleppo, orphanages were established by priests such as Hovaness Eskijian and the Swiss missionary Sister Beatrice Rohner. In the greater region, the Near East Relief organization founded orphanages, hospitals, and refugee camps and sponsored food, clothing, and medical supply drives through direct appeal to the American public. But by 1917 the Ottomans had closed down most aid efforts within their borders. Aleppo's international orphanages were replaced with ones run by the state only for those young enough not to remember their Armenian identity. A lucky few, like Shahen, Sosi, and Mariam, were hidden by families of Arabs and Kurds and even Turks like Mustafa. While Ottoman authorities used a rhetoric of *jihad* to incite the murder of Armenians, the sharif of Mecca called for Muslims to save them. After the war ended, Near East Relief continued their work, ultimately saving the lives of 132,000 orphans.

One of the largest of the Near East Relief orphanages was located in Gyumri, a city that sits on the closed border between present-day Turkey and Armenia. From 1918 to 1920, Armenia briefly had the status of an independent republic. According to the Treaty of Sèvres, signed by the Ottoman government and the Allied powers in 1920, this republic was to include much of the land that is eastern Turkey today. Turkish nationalists under the leadership of Kemal Attatürk opposed this treaty; war erupted, and the fledgling republic collapsed. What remained of Armenia was absorbed into the Soviet Union. On September 21, 1991, Armenia declared its independence from the Soviet Union. This small nation has remained independent since then.

I took a bit of purposeful poetic license with a few facts. In this story, Ardziv calls the Ottoman Turks "drum caps," identifying them by the felted fezzes they wore. Though the fez was certainly part of the Ottoman army uniform, Armenians also wore these stylish hats at the beginning of the twentieth century. We mongrels know that identity lives in social surfaces.

And what of people who marry across social boundaries, as did Anahid and Asan? In 1914, the lives of Armenians, Kurds, and Turks near Palu were socially intertwined. The rare "love matches" that undoubtedly occurred contrast with the many acts of violence committed against women during the genocide. Some Kurdish groups were well known for helping and hiding Armenians.

Genocide, the systematic extermination of one people by another, always includes a phase of dehumanization that links those who will be eliminated with animals, diseases, vermin—things humans have permission to kill. Genocide ends when denial ends. Healing involves finding our shared humanity, achieving justice for the harm done, and finding the space in our hearts to forgive.

Acknowledgments

Though always a voracious reader, I came to writing late. Writing is never a solitary act, but depends upon the insights and responses of others. I have been fortunate to have such varied, wise, and generous others in my life.

My first forays into creative writing were sustained by writing retreats filled with conversations about craft. Heartfelt thanks to Mary Atkinson, Franny Billingsley, Toni Buzzeo, Jennifer Jacobson, Sarah Lamstein, Cindy Lord, and Carol Peacock for inspiration and guidance, and for sacred writing time and space. Sarah Aaronson, Katie Bayrel, Ann Cardinal, Nicole Griffin, Kate Hosford, Daphne Kalmar, Adi Rule, and Zu Vincent gave me the faith to continue to revise with the benefit of their insights. From the earliest drafts to the work that this book is now, Jacqueline Davies was my trusted reader and friend.

Sharing writing with Burlington area poets/writers Sarah Bartlett, Sue Burton, Jaina Clough, Lee Ann Cox, Stephen Cramer, Sharyl Green, Marilyn Grigas, Laban Hill, Major Jackson, Jill Leininger, Melissa Pasanen, Grace Per Lee, and Liz Powell shaped the lines of this book. Special thanks to Adrie Kusserow, who also inhabits that liminal territory between anthropology and creative writing, and to Beebe Bahrami, who long ago inspired me to enter that space.

Vermont College of Fine Arts transformed me into a writer. Four brilliant advisors—Julie Larios, Tim Wynne-Jones, Rita Williams-Garcia, and Margaret Bechard—mentored me with unparalleled generosity and rigor. Thanks to my stellar workshop faculty, Kathi Appelt, Alan Cumyn, Louise Hawes, Uma Krishnaswami, and Martine Leavitt; my workshop mates; the members of my class, all of whom "keep the story;" and to Jane Resh Thomas, who propelled me toward the program. Every lecture, reading, and moment at VCFA was a gift.

Friends nurtured me throughout this journey, each with their special gifts. Thanks to Emmanuelle Dobbs for always valuing my *"arménianité,"* and to the Manuelyan family, Hasmik Baghramyan, and the members of Lokum for helping me hang on to it in northern Vermont. Thanks to Fletcher Boote, Paula Duncan, Mary Hill, Jill Lyons, Polly Menendez, Yvette Pigeon, Dianne Shullenberger, Janet Van Fleet, and Martha Whitney for movement, flow, and voice, and to Robert Lair for the abundant tulips.

My Vanetsi brother and genocide scholar, Dr. Harutyun Marutyan, opened doors in Armenia for me and was always ready for a deep conversation about the place of art in social change. Dr. Hayk Demoyan graciously welcomed me into the research library and the community of scholars at the Armenian Genocide Museum and Institute in Yerevan. He, along with Asya Darbinyan, Hasmik Grigoryan, Gohar Khanumyan, Mihran Minassian, and Naira Melisetyan, was particularly helpful as I researched the details of this story. Any errors that remain are mine alone. Thanks to Dr. Vahé Tachjian, who directs Houshamadyan, a remarkable reconstruction of life in the Ottoman Empire in 1914. Dr. Rubina Peroomian of UCLA generously shared her wisdom and knowledge with me. Dr. Rouben Galichian kindly shared period maps and his expertise on maps of the region with me. Anna Berberyan and her dance group welcomed me into their midst, shaping the music and dance threads of this story (*Shad shnorhagalutyun, Bari Khoomp!*). Vahan Bournazian guided me on details of Armenian grape growing and connected me with the haunting music of Palu. Through her efforts to improve my Armenian handwriting, Anahit Avetisyan inspired little Mariam to write. I am indebted to the Fulbright Scholar Program, the Vermont Studio Center, Vermont College of Fine Arts, the Vermont Arts Council, and the National Endowment for the Arts for support while I worked on this book.

Agent extraordinaire Ammi Joan Paquette believed in this book and found such a good home for it. Editor Michelle Poploff always asked just the right questions with perfect timing, clarity, and grace. Her unwavering commitment to the hard truths of this subject kept me safe as I wrote. Special thanks to Rebecca Short for the kindest constancy, and to Alison Impey, Heather Kelly, Colleen Fellingham, Laura Antonacci, Beverly Horowitz, and the rest of the superb team at Delacorte Press for sustaining the story's spirit through every phase of production.

My parents, Alice and David Walrath, imparted their

love of books to me, a gift that outlasts a lifetime. My sister, Suzy Walrath Mehrotra; my mother's sister, Rose Robischon; and her cousin, Toros Hovivian, gave me love and solid memories, and Aunt Sona Takoushjian shared the wonders of her kitchen and other arts. I am especially grateful to my three sons, Nishan, Tavid, and Aram, for countless precious moments and for the person each of you has become. And above all, my dear husband, Peter Bingham, has been with me every step of every journey and makes the magic of the *oud* sing wherever we are.

Glossary

Alashkerti kochari (ah-lash-KER-tee KOH-char-ee):
The kochari is a series of line dances that includes lots of knee movements. It is popular with Armenians, Assyrians, Greeks, and Kurds. In the version from the western Armenian village of Alashkert, men link arm to waist and "fly" as they support one another, moving quickly to a haunting *duduk* melody.

alik (AH-leek): The Armenian word for "wave."

anoush (AH-noosh): The Armenian word for "sweet." Also a girl's name.

ardziv (ar-DZIV): The Armenian word for "eagle."

astidjan (AH-stih-DJAHN): The Armenian word for "step."

ayran (ai-RAHN): The Turkish word for a cool drink made from watery yogurt.

baba (BAH-bah): The Arabic word for "dad."

baran (bah-RAHN): The Armenian word for rows of grapes in a vineyard; used as a unit of measure.

baron (bah-ROHN): The Armenian title used to show respect for a man.

bastegh (BAH-stegh): A sweet made from cooked fruits spread into thin sheets.

basturma (BAHST-oor-mah): A dried, spiced meat.

charukh (CHAR-ookh): A simple shoe consisting of a thick piece of leather pierced with holes for thick leather laces that bind them to the wearer's feet.

chetes (CHEH-tez): Killing squads of criminals, generally of Kurdish origin, released from prison to carry out the Ottoman policy of extermination.

choor (chure): The Armenian word for "water."

Der Hayr (der hire): A married priest in the Armenian church.

digin (dee-GEEN): The Armenian term of respect for a woman. *Gin* means "woman."

dolma (DOHL-mah): The word used throughout the region for savory foods such as grape leaves, peppers, eggplant, tomatoes, and cabbage, stuffed with rice and/or ground meat and other vegetables and spices, served hot or cold.

door (dure): The Armenian command for "you give." *Choor door* means "Give me water."

duduk (DOO-dook): A double-reed wind instrument made from the wood of an apricot tree. The name *duduk* comes from Turkish. The traditional Armenian name was *tsirana-pogh,* meaning "apricot horn."

dumbek (DOOM-bek): A goblet-shaped hand drum made of metal, clay, or wood, usually with a goatskin head. Its name comes from Arabic.

gavour (GAH-voor): The Turkish word for "infidel" (one without faith), used as an epithet against Christians in the Ottoman Empire.

goozem (goo-ZEHM): "I want" in western Armenian.

halva (HAHL-vah): A dense sweet made of sesame paste, butter, and sugar.

hijab (hee-JAHB): The head scarf worn by some Muslim women.

hos egoor (hos eh-GOOR): The western Armenian phrase "come" (*egoor*) "here" (*hos*).

jagadakirus (djah-GAHD a KEER-uhs): The Armenian phrase meaning "my fate," literally "written" (*krel*, to write) "on the forehead" (*djagad*). The *-s* ending indicates the first person.

jan (djahn): The Armenian term of endearment, used after names constantly in everyday speech.

jbid (zhuh-BEED): The Armenian word for "smile."

jori/joreni (ZHOH-ri/ZHOH-ren-i): Armenian words (among others) for "persimmon tree."

kabalak (KAH-bah-lahk): A somewhat conical cloth-wrapped helmet with a chin strap modeled after a Black Sea hat, introduced to Ottoman troops by Enver Pasha in 1914.

kadayif (kah-DYE-eef): A dessert made with shredded phyllo dough and ground nuts.

keffiyeh (keh-FEE-uh): The head scarf worn by Arab men, sometimes tied and sometimes draped and secured with a braided ring.

keri (KEH-ree): The Armenian word for a maternal uncle. A paternal uncle is a *horyeghpayr* (father's brother).

kilim (KIH-lim): Flat tapestry-woven carpets that are distinct from thicker knotted carpets.

koonuh (KOO-nuh): The Armenian word for "the sleep." *Koon* is "sleep"; the *-uh* suffix is the definite article.

lahmajoon (LAH-mah-joon): A very thin flat bread covered with meat, vegetables, and spices.

madzoon (MAH-dzoon): The Armenian word for "yogurt," often considered a source of longevity.

mahlap (MAH-lahp): A spice made from ground cherry seeds.

manti (MAHN-tee): Dumplings made of dough stuffed with ground meat and spices, baked and then served in a broth and topped with a yogurt and garlic sauce.

maqam (MAH-kahm): A musical mode or scale structure used in the music of the Middle East, Central Asia, and North Africa.

meg (meg): The Armenian word for the number one.

mizrap (MEEZ-rahp): A five-inch-long flexible pick used to play the *oud,* a string instrument. The traditional eagle quill has been replaced by plastic.

oud (OOD): A fretless eleven-stringed instrument with a large oval chamber that is the precursor to the European lute. The word *lute* comes from the Arabic *al oud.*

Soorp Hayr (sourp highr): The name for celibate priests, literally "holy father."

tamzara (TAHM-zah-rah): An Anatolian line or circle folk dance in a 9/8 rhythm that includes stomping at the end of each phrase, symbolizing stomping away all bad things.

tan (tahn): The Armenian word for a cool drink made of watery yogurt.

teshekkur ederim (TESH-eh-kiur eh-DEH-rum): The Turkish word for "thank you."

thobe (tob): The traditional long, loose robe worn by Arab men.

tonir (TOH-neer): The traditional underground wood-fired clay oven for baking Armenian flat bread (*lavash*). In western Armenian towns and villages such as Palu, each home had its own *tonir.*

trchoon (tur-CHOON): The Armenian word for "bird."

yalla (yal-lah): The Arabic phrase meaning "let's go" or "come on."

yerek (yeh-REK): The Armenian word for the number three.

yergoo (yer-GOOH): The Armenian word for the number two.

zurna (ZUHR-nah): A double-reed woodwind instrument made of apricot wood with a bell-shaped base that has a piercing oboelike sound.

Resources

NONFICTION

Akçam, Taner. *The Young Turks' Crime Against Humanity: The Armenian Genocide and Ethnic Cleansing in the Ottoman Empire.* Princeton: Princeton University Press, 2012.

The Armenian Genocide Museum Institute, National Academy of Sciences of the Republic of Armenia. genocide-museum.am.

Armenian Genocide Resource Library for Teachers. teachgenocide .org.

Armenian National Institute. armenian-genocide.org.

Auron, Yair. *The Banality of Denial.* New Brunswick, NJ: Transaction, 2003.

Balakian, Peter. *The Burning Tigris: The Armenian Genocide and America's Response.* New York: Harper Collins, 2004.

Dadrian, Vahakn. *The History of the Armenian Genocide: Ethnic Conflict from the Balkans to Anatolia to the Caucasus.* Providence/Oxford: Berghahn Books, 1995.

The Genocide Education Project. genocideeducation.org.

Houshamadyan: A Project to Reconstruct Ottoman Armenian Town and Village Life, houshamadyan.org/en/home.html.

Hovannisian, Richard. *The Armenian Genocide: Cultural and Ethical Legacies.* New Brunswick, NJ: Transaction, 2007.

Kaiser, Hilmar. *At the Crossroads of Der Zor: Death, Survival, and Humanitarian Resistance in Aleppo, 1915–1917.* Princeton: Gomidas Press, 2002.

Kévorkian, Raymond. *The Armenian Genocide: A Complete History.* London: I. B. Tauris, 2011.

Miller, Donald E., and Lorna Touryan Miller. *Survivors: An Oral History of the Armenian Genocide.* Berkeley: University of California Press, 1993.

Stanton, Gregory H. *The Eight Stages of Genocide.* A briefiing for the U.S. State Department in 1996. genocidewatch.org/aboutgenocide /8stagesofgenocide.html.

Suny, Ronald Grigor, Fatma Muge Gocek, and Norman M. Naimar. *A Question of Genocide: Armenians and Turks at the End of the Ottoman Empire.* New York: Oxford University Press, 2011.

Totten, Samuel. *Teaching About Genocide: Issues, Approaches, and Resources.* Greenwich, CT: Information Age Publishing, 2006.

Üngör, Uğur Ümit, and Mehmet Polatel. *Confiscation and Destruction: The Young Turk Seizure of Armenian Property.* London/New York: Continuum, 2011.

MEMOIRS

Arlen, Michael J. *Passage to Ararat.* New York: Farrar, Straus & Giroux, 1975.

Balakian, Peter. *Black Dog of Fate.* New York: Basic Books, 1997.

Çetin, Fetihye. *My Grandmother: An Armenian-Turkish Memoir.* New York: Verso, 2012.

Hovannisian, Garin K. *Family of Shardows: A Century of Murder, Memory, and the Armenian American Dream.* New York: Harper Collins, 2010.

Mardiganian, Aurora. *Ravished Armenia: The Story of Aurora Mardiganian, the Christian Girl Who Lived Through the Great Massacres*. New York: Kingfield Press, 1918.

Morgenthau, Henry. *Ambassador Morgenthau's Story*. New York: Doubleday, 1918.

FICTION

Bagdasarian, Adam. *Forgotten Fire*. New York: Dell Laurel-Leaf, 2000.

Bohjalian, Chris. *The Sandcastle Girls*. New York: Random House, 2012.

Edgarian, Carol. *Rise the Euphrates*. New York: Random House, 1994.

Kherdian, David. *A Road from Home*. New York: Greenwillow, 1988.

Marcom, Micheline Aharonian. *Three Apples Fell from Heaven*. New York: Riverhead Books, 2001.

Pamuk, Orhan. *Snow*. London: Faber and Faber, 2004.

Saroyan, William. *My Name Is Aram*. New York: Harcourt Brace, 1940.

Saroyan, William. "Seventy Thousand Assyrians," from *The Daring Young Man on the Flying Trapeze*. New York: Harcourt Brace, 1934.

Shafak, Elif. *The Bastard of Istanbul*. New York: Viking, 2007.

Werfel, Franz. *The Forty Days of Musa Dagh*. New York: Viking, 1934.

FEATURE FILMS

Ararat. Directed by Atom Egoyan, 2002.

The Color of Pomegranates. Directed by Sergei Parajanov, 1968.

Three Apples Fell from Heaven. Directed by Shekhar Kapur, forthcoming 2015.

POEMS, MUSIC, AND ART

Aram Khachaturian (composer)
khachaturian.am/eng/biography.htm

Arshile Gorky (painter)
Taylor, Michael R., ed. *Arshile Gorky: A Retrospective.* Philadelphia: Philadelphia Museum of Art Publications, 2009.

Diana Der-Hovanessian (poet)
Selected Poems. Rhinebeck, New York: Sheep Meadow Press, 1994.

Gomidas Vartabed (composer)

Bayrakdarian, Isabel. *Gomidas Songs.* Nonesuch Recordings, 2008.

Kuyumjian, Rita Soulahian. *Archaeology of Madness: Komitas, Portrait of an Armenian Icon.* London: Gomidas Institute, 2010.

Hovhaness Tumanyan (poet, writer)
armenianhouse.org/tumanyan/bio-en.html

Martiros Saryan (painter)

Khachatrian, S. *M. Saryan: Selected Works.* Moscow: Sovetsky Khudozhnik Publishers, 1983.

Martiros Saryan. Masters of World Painting. Leningrad: Aurora Art Publications, 1975.

Siamanto (poet)
"The Dance." umd.umich.edu/dept/armenian/literatu/dance .html